The Caribbean Castaway

Michael Richardson

Contents

Chapter 1

S IX MONTHS AGO

On the salty, sea-smelling streets of Key Largo, just a few miles north of Sexton Cove, a tall youth walked aimlessly toward the end of a dock. He swallowed another bite of fish before stuffing the rest in his back pocket, making sure it was carefully preserved in a clean plastic baggie. The soles of his feet were charcoal-black and grimy as he stood on the edge of the dock. The young man, his face covered in stubble and matted with dirt, studied the rippling ocean with frustration. His irritation soon gave way to a guarded expression as he watched two bowriders and a small fishing boat glide across the water. He needed to get away.

The nearest restaurant, however, was miles down the Overseas Highway, and the youth was tired of walking. He was weary of hitchhiking and staying out of sight of cops and living on his own.

He glanced across the water at the Anchorage Resort and Yacht Club. People milled about on the docks and talked excitedly as they strolled inside the building. The youth yawned and headed back down the dock. He whistled a tune and shoved his hands into his pockets, trying not to think about food or walking or the ocean. There was only his tattered clothing, his bare feet, and the miles of empty road ahead of him.

Two men peered out of the safety of their fishing boat to watch the tall youth. The edge of a plastic baggie sticking out of his back pocket was barely visible, as were the stained soles of his feet.

"Is that him?" one of the men asked in a low voice.

"Yeah, Sully, that's him," said the second, his words laced with a thick Spanish accent. They set down their binoculars in unison when the youth disappeared down the dock, out of view.

The man named Sully picked up his radio. "We got him," was all he said before clicking off. The Spaniard started the engine and gave his partner a thin smile.

"It won't be long now, amigo."

Chapter 2

"For your homework, I want you to take some pictures this weekend using reflectors, diffusers, or filters like we learned in class today. Play around with various qualities of light. I suggest you take still photos rather than action sequences, as you can take time to adjust..."

Hayley sighed and tuned out the rest of Mr. McCarthy's instructions. She busied herself by placing her camera around her neck and readjusting her ear buds. After stuffing her remaining papers and binders inside her backpack, she slung it over one shoulder and waited impatiently for Mr. McCarthy to finish.

"...due next Wednesday, so I suggest you get started this weekend before we begin our next project." Finally running out of instructions to give, the teacher clapped his hands and said, "Alright, see you next week. Class is dismissed."

The room suddenly came alive with murmuring and shuffling of feet. Hayley stood up and wound her way through the crowds of students out the door. She automatically made a beeline for the staircase. A song by Odesza, blasting through her buds, drowned out the loud chattering of students in the hall. Hayley hadn't made it two more steps before someone suddenly grabbed her arm.

"What?" she asked, turning around. She yanked out one of her ear buds, but the frown on her face immediately morphed into a slight smile when she saw who it was. "Oh, Oliver. Hey."

"Hayley! Uh, hi," the tall, lanky boy stammered. He readjusted his thin rectangular glasses.

"Is there anything I can do for you?"

"Nope." Oliver smiled goofily. Realizing his mistake, he quickly added, "Actually, I mean, if you're not busy this weekend, I was thinking we could work on the project. You know, all those lighting techniques and stuff. I have a hard time remembering certain things, but you—"

"Oliver," Hayley laughed, "you have a ninety-eight percent in our photography course. That's probably the highest grade out of all McCarthy's classes." She chuckled again. "You told me yourself, remember? I'm sure you can do the project on your own. In fact, you're probably better off without me."

"Oh." His face fell. "Right. Um, I guess you're busy this weekend, then?"

Hayley thought for a second. "I'm visiting my Gran." She nodded and smiled, then readjusted her backpack. She fingered the camera around her neck before taking a few steps backwards. "Well, I'll see you on Monday, Oliver."

"Okay. I mean—yes. Monday." He ducked his head and quickly vanished into the crowd, leaving Hayley with a lingering smile on her face. She laughed quietly and headed downstairs to the exit. It wasn't that she disliked Oliver; he was just...annoying. Hayley preferred to be alone while working on projects, while Oliver was an awkward geek looking for conversation—at least, that was how she saw him. They exchanged an occasional word in class, but that was all.

After glancing from side to side and crossing the street, Hayley entered the large parking structure outside of Florida International University. She wasted no time in finding her car and zipping out on the main highway that would take her to her home in Palmetto Bay. Though she wasn't a fast driver, usually it only took her 20 minutes to make the 15-mile drive from FIU to her small apartment.

Before long, the heavy traffic and large buildings of the University disappeared from Hayley's rearview mirror. She happily rolled down her window, rested one arm on the door, and let the cool Florida breeze blow her stress away. It was officially the weekend—no more tests, no more classes, and no more worrying about college. It was time to relax.

With her camera still dangling around her neck, Hayley cranked up the radio and settled back in her seat. She hummed along to the music the entire drive home.

Hayley grunted as she groped for her keys in her pocket. "A-ha," she declared, pulling out her set of keys. She smiled with relief, unlocked her door, and stepped inside.

Her apartment was small but cozy. It was the perfect size for a college student like herself: one bedroom, one kitchen, one bathroom, and one dining/living room. It was all squished into half the size of a normal house, but that didn't bother Hayley. It was far better than the alternative.

After tossing her backpack onto the kitchen counter, Hayley poured herself a glass of lemonade—making sure to stir in extra sugar—and gently placed her camera on her bed. As soon as her glass was emptied, she rinsed the cup in the sink and headed out the door. She locked her apartment behind her, took one step to the right, and knocked on the adjacent door.

"Hey, it's me," she called.

A few seconds later, a gravelly voice replied, "Come on in, sweetie."

Hayley smiled and pushed the door open. Immediately, the soft sound of jazz music and the smell of fresh fruit touched her senses. "Hi Gran. How've you been?"

"Oh, fine." Gran's gray-white hair was pulled back into its usual bun. She was wearing her favorite pink-checkered apron as she sliced bananas and tossed the pieces into a large fruit salad.

Hayley hungrily stepped up to the bowl and pinched a strawberry between two fingers. "Do you mind?" she asked.

"Go right ahead, sweetie. I'm not eating all this fruit by myself." Gran chuckled and opened a can of mandarin oranges.

Hayley waited patiently as Gran finished slicing the rest of the fruit and untied her apron. "It's delicious," she declared.

"I thought it would go perfect with an episode of The Twilight Zone," Gran said with a smile. "Can you help me carry this bowl to the living room?"

Hayley quickly reached out and grabbed the large bowl of fruit salad. "Go ahead and take a seat. I got it." She followed the elderly woman to the couch, where they both plopped down and Hayley placed the fruit bowl on top of the coffee table. In a few moments, Gran used her extra large remote to get TiVo working, and The Twilight Zone appeared on the small screen in front of them.

"Have you thought about getting a hi-def TV?" Hayley asked carefully.

"Nope," Gran said without missing a beat.

"But everyone has them. You'll be amazed when you see how clear these new TVs are."

Gran shushed her and took a mandarin orange from the bowl. "The show's starting."

Hayley rolled her eyes and smiled. It was an ongoing battle between her and Gran to get her to buy a new TV. The old, flickering square one she had used for the past four decades was inconsequential compared to the awesome hi-def televisions today. Hayley knew it was only a matter of time before she—or the outdated TV—would force Gran to give in.

But for now, it was okay. With a slice of banana in one hand and Gran's leathery fingers in the other, Hayley settled back into the old couch and watched as Rod Serling came onto the TV, a lighted cigarette between his lips. She was grateful for life just the way it was.

Chapter 3

SIX MONTHS AGO

The young man felt pain before he even saw it coming. He staggered backwards as another blow was delivered to his face. He hit the deck of the boat and immediately tasted blood. Hoots and whistles erupted from the ring of men surrounding him.

"You wanna tell us now?" the youth's accoster growled, leering over him. The man's muscular form blocked the sizzling Florida sun from the youth's vision, and the youth took that moment to catch his breath. He squinted up through two newly-formed black eyes.

"Answer me!" the man demanded.

In response, the youth arched his back and spit in his face. A gross mixture of saliva and blood ran down the man's chin. He wiped it off with the back of his hand and glared at his victim. "That wasn't so smart, Jack," he growled. "Or should I say...Jack Nau." Lifting his knee, he drove his foot hard into Jack's stomach. Jack immediately felt the wind get knocked out of him, and he gasped for breath. His head swam.

"Come on, Clyde," the Spaniard said. "I think that's enough."

"Shut up," Clyde snarled. He wiped the blood off his knuckles.

"The kid's not talkin'. What if he's telling the truth? What if he doesn't know where it is?"

"Oh, he knows where it is, all right." Clyde laughed slowly and murderously. "And he's going to tell me one of these days, even if I have to give him a little motivation first." He leered over Jack once more, a sinister smile on his twisted face. "Isn't that right, Jack?"

Jack closed his eyes and tried to ignore the chuckles of the men surrounding him. It had been four days since they caught him—four long, torturous days. But no matter what he said, they never believed him.

"Pick him up," Clyde ordered.

Two men stepped forward and slung their arms underneath Jack's, lifting him off the deck. Jack's head lolled to one side as he fought to remain conscious. His face was covered in bruises and blood, and when Clyde walked over to the railing, Jack swore he saw three of him.

"See that horizon over there, Jack?" Clyde nodded in the direction of the vast ocean, his lips curling into a smirk. "We're giving you one more day. This is your last chance to tell us where it is, or we get rid of you."

Jack licked his bloody lips and did his best to remain upright. Get rid of me?

"The Caribbean is littered with islands. You know that well enough. There's the Florida Keys, the Bahamas, the Virgin Islands..." With every syllable, Clyde inched closer to Jack until he was breathing down the youth's neck. "But you know what?" he snarled. "If you don't tell me where that map is by this time tomorrow, you're gonna be stuck on one of those pitiful little islands. And I'll make sure it's an island far away from any shipping lanes, way out in the middle of the Caribbean where you can never leave. You got that?"

Jack told his limbs to do something—anything—to hurt Clyde, but it was in vain. He was frozen. Just as his puffy eyelids closed and his mind succumbed to unconsciousness, he got a glimpse of Clyde's leering face. "It's up to you, Jack," he said with a sneer. "Your fate is all up to you."

Chapter 4

P RESENT DAY

During the last few minutes of her college algebra test, Hayley doodled in her notebook and waited for the remaining students to finish. She paused after completing a drawing of a hibiscus flower and chewed on the end of her pencil. She only had one more class before the school day was over: photography. It seemed like Mondays always went by the slowest—especially math classes on Monday. Hayley frowned and twirled her pencil in between her fingers. At least there's only one week to go until spring break.

Finally, as the last seconds of the clock ticked down, Mr. Yeoman called for all the tests to be passed up. Hayley slung her backpack over one shoulder and fingered the camera dangling around her neck. As soon as class was dismissed, she made a beeline for the opposite side of the school. Already she walked with a lighter spring in her step as she anticipated her favorite and most relaxing period out of the school day.

Before she even made it to the door of her photography class, however, she stopped when she heard a familiar voice call her name.

"Hayley!" A tall, lanky boy wearing rectangular glasses came into view. His goofy smile made his features seem even more boyish than usual.

"Hi, Oliver."

"You're in Mr. Yeoman's class, right?"

She cocked her head to one side. "How'd you know that?"

"I s-saw you walk out just a few minutes ago. I have his class on Tuesdays. Tuesdays and Thursdays."

"Oh. Good luck on the test tomorrow, then."

Oliver's squinted at her through his glasses. "W-was it hard?"

"A little. There were a few logarithms I had some trouble with, but it wasn't too bad."

"I'm not very good at math."

"That's okay." Hayley gave him a reassuring smile, though she detected something in his eyes. "I've always taken you for the type of guy who likes math. I guess I was wrong."

"Yeah." He grinned. "I guess you were."

Hayley nodded and turned to walk into the classroom, a little unnerved by the way he was staring at her. She blushed and ducked her head.

"Wait, Hayley!"

She paused. "Yeah?"

"Uh, do you think I could...um...call you later? If I have questions about the math test?"

She gave him a look, not entirely sure what he was getting at. "Isn't there someone in your class you could—"

"No."

"Oh. Okay, then." After a few seconds' deliberation, Hayley nodded and gave Oliver a brief smile. "Let me give you my number."

Oliver sighed with relief as he took out his phone and punched in her number. "Th-thanks so much, Hayley. You're a lifesaver."

"No problem." She turned and took an extra-long stride into the classroom, determined not to be held back a third time. She sat down in the front corner of the class, where she was boxed in by three other students. She didn't raise her head as Oliver trailed into the room, flickering his gaze over to where she was seated. Out of her peripheral vision, Hayley saw him give a sad glance in her direction before sitting down in an empty seat on the opposite side of the room.

She slid lower into her seat. She felt a little guilty about ditching Oliver like that, but she regretted giving him her number. Though she did need help with math, she had a feeling nothing good would come of having a direct connection to Oliver.

But *he's nice*, she reasoned with herself. *He just has a crush on you. What's the harm in being nice in return?*

Hayley groaned and tried to hide behind the frizzy-haired student next to her when Oliver glanced in her direction. She averted her eyes. *Because I don't want to give him the wrong idea.*

Chapter 5

T WO MONTHS AGO

In the dim, flickering glow of his campfire, Jack settled back against the cave wall, stroking his beard and staring at the glistening rock across from him through the flames. Four letters had been carved out of the stone, followed by a tally of the 93 days he had been on this Godforsaken island in the middle of nowhere.

He frowned at the tally marks, then at the letters. J-A-C-K, they spelled. "Jack," the youth murmured to himself, his voice cracking from disuse. "Jack Patterson. That's my name. Or is it?" He squinted through the flames once more until his eyes began to water. He blinked rapidly and rubbed his eyes with his knuckles.

Suddenly, the cave seemed to be flooded with light. He froze with his hands near his face. A luminous blur of words and images flashed across his eyes, and then they were gone. The flickering fire was the only source of light once again.

Jack shuddered. That wasn't the first time something like that had happened. The "incidents," as he liked to call them, were few and far between. As the soothing sound of waves, crackling firewood, and hum of insects lulled him to sleep,

Jack's head began to nod and the incident quickly vanished from his mind. He fell into a dreamless slumber.

The next morning, Jack awoke to blinding sunlight and the last traces of smoke from his campfire. He rubbed the sleep from his eyes and groggily sat upright, his back scratchy from leaning against the crude wall of the cave. As soon as he stopped yawning and felt slightly more awake, he grabbed his makeshift dagger—a skinny rock he had whittled to a point—and scratched one more tally into the wall across from him.

With that done, Jack set out to do his daily activities. 94 days of solitary living on an island about a mile long as it was wide left very little for him to do. He consoled himself through his routines. That was the one thing that kept him sane and breathing.

First, he washed himself in the freshwater spring next to his cave. After hanging his wet clothes on an overhanging tree branch, he used a sharp piece of flint to keep his beard nice and trim—at least, about as trim as he could with such crude resources. With the hot Caribbean sun beating down on his back, he headed across the island to its jungle-infested side. There was nothing but vegetation on the south end, where Jack's cave was, but the north end grew thick with palm trees and foliage. As soon as Jack reached the beginning of the jungle, he climbed up a half-bent palm tree and began gathering coconuts.

Coconut-gathering took a few hours' time—about forty-five minutes to gather and the rest to break them open.

After making several trips back to his cave, Jack finished the coconut part of his routine and headed back to the beach.

Now it was time to fish. Though he wasn't an expert spear fisher, he always came home with at least one fresh catch before the sun was three-quarters' way overhead. Using another makeshift dagger attached to a strong branch by vines, he slaved away under the sun until he had three decent-sized fish under his arm.

Now hot, exhausted and sweaty, Jack set the fish back down in his cave on some palm fronds to dry. He peeled off his shirt, which was as dirty and worn as his jeans, and made his final trek to the beach. The day was finally cooling off now that the sun had passed its zenith, and Jack always looked forward to his afternoon swim. He rolled up his jeans as far as they would go and dashed into the surf.

Jack had always been a strong swimmer, but he wasn't strong enough to swim to the nearest island. There was nothing but blue Caribbean waters all around him, and the blazing sun in the sky to keep him company. He hadn't the faintest idea how to build a raft, either. Escape was practically impossible.

After swimming a half-mile parallel to the shore, Jack felt refreshed and cooled off. He retreated back to the beach and took a seat in the shade of an overgrown dwarf palm. He had five more hours before it grew dark, which left him more than enough time to go fruit-picking and do his daily exercises.

Jack grunted as he began his set of push-ups. Midway through his workout, several thoughts crossed his mind:

Why do I keep doing this? Why am I staying in shape? What's the purpose?

"Because," he said to himself as he finished his last round of sit-ups, "someday, when I get off this island, I'm going to be thankful that I'm alive and kicking."

Maybe that was the hope he clung to. Maybe that was why he slaved away under the hot Caribbean sun for hours and hours, only to retreat back to his cave and carve one more tally mark onto the wall. Maybe that was why he held on to the burning hatred for the men who had put him on this island—the men he hadn't seen in over three months.

Jack's eyebrows narrowed in concentration as he started his nightly fire. As soon as the first log was set ablaze, the rest were soon consumed in fire, and the warmth radiated onto Jack's salt-covered skin. He sighed and leaned back against the cave wall, watching the last glimpses of the sun as it sank below the horizon. He was full from his catch of fish and a few slices of fruit—his usual dinner. After gulping down the last of his coconut water, he made one more trip to the freshwater spring before going to bed.

Jack had a fleeting thought of what he could do to escape. Though he hadn't seen one boat since he had arrived on the island, he knew they were out there. People were out there. Civilization was out there—a civilization he hadn't seen in three months.

But even three months could feel like an eternity.

I could build a fire, Jack thought. A smoke signal. But the thought was dashed to pieces when his right thigh began to throb. He could feel the eight-inch scar through the thin material of his jeans; a scar given to him by the men who had put him on this island. The last time he had used a smoke signal to try to alert passing ships, the men had returned with a warning and a slice to his leg. "Don't try it again," they ordered. "You're only allowed to have a fire at night. Is that clear?"

To Jack, it was crystal. There were ten of them and only one of him. Though he still didn't know how they had found him wandering along the coast of Florida, he knew why they had come. He knew why they had abandoned him. The reason was obvious, but the intent of their kidnapping was the real question. Now that they had Jack where they wanted him, why was he still alive? Why did his island happen to have all the necessary materials for survival, yet when Jack tried to get away, he was told he couldn't?

It puzzled him. But it also fueled him with a passion and determination like no other. He would get off the island. He would.

Chapter 6

PRESENT DAY

Looming over the cracked sidewalk were rows of jacaranda trees, their white gnarled limbs stretching over the street and front yards of neighborhood houses. Hayley's legs were on fire as she sprinted the last block, throwing her head back and getting a glimpse of the warm sun through the purple jacaranda flowers. Once she reached the corner, she slowed to a jog, allowing herself to cool down before turning onto the adjacent street.

Hayley wiped the sweat from her brow and shook out her legs. She always felt oddly satisfied after a hard run. She tried to run at least 20 miles every week with a few sprints in between to stay in shape. She had joined a community gym a few months ago, but she found jogging on a treadmill obnoxiously boring compared to dashing down vibrant neighborhoods and over various terrain.

As soon as she reached her apartment, she grabbed her keys from where they were tied into the laces of her running shoes and unlocked the door. After drinking a large amount of water, she felt refreshed and rehydrated. She retied her messy bun and decided to check in on Gran.

She entered her grandmother's apartment still in her spandex and frumpy T-shirt. "Hey Gran," she called loudly, announcing her presence.

"I'm in the living room," came the reply.

Hayley plopped down on the couch next to her grandmother, watching as Gran never once looked away from the travel magazine in her aged hands.

"Whatcha got there?" Hayley asked curiously, leaning forward to see the interior of the magazine.

"I'm doing research," Gran said swiftly. "Very important research. You're not going to believe what I've found."

Hayley raised an eyebrow. She normally didn't hear that tone in Gran's voice. It was one of sheer determination, a sharp contrast to the easygoing grandmother she knew. She shifted in her seat to get a better look. "What kind of research?"

Gran slapped the magazine closed. "I can't tell you."

The response came as a surprise. "Why not?" Hayley exclaimed.

"Because I'm not finished yet." Gran smiled and laughed softly. "And I don't think I can stand to sit next to you much longer, honey. It would do you good to take a shower."

Hayley chuckled. She could take a hint. "All right, I'll be back in a few."

"Want to do a Costco run when you get back? I feel like nibbling on some free samples."

"Sure," Hayley called on her way out the door. She glanced over her shoulder and saw Gran pick up the magazine once again. She frowned and hurried into her own apartment, curiosity piqued. Gran was determined to do something, and Hayley wanted to find out what it was.

Chapter 7

ONE MONTH AGO

Jack's arms ached as he trudged out of the water, his back slicked with saltwater and his limbs exhausted from swimming against the current. He collapsed in the cool sand and let the warm sunrays hit his bare skin. It felt heavenly.

He stared up at the leafy palm fronds fluttering above him. Suddenly, his nose twitched when an insect landed directly between his eyes. Jack frowned and brushed it off, going cross-eyed for a few seconds and laughing in spite of himself. His breath caught when another jumble of words and images flashed before him. There was the light, that odd combination of symbols and random letters. It vanished just as quickly as it had arrived.

Jack blinked a few times and willed his breathing to return to normal. He fought to remember any of the letters or images, but nothing came to mind. It was like the incident had never occurred. Strange...

After relaxing in the sun for a while, Jack found himself nodding off, and he slowly sat up until his equilibrium came back to normal. He watched the ocean in silent fascination for a few minutes, with its crashing waves the only sound.

He pictured a boat, a small dot on the horizon, coming closer and closer. He imagined people—people other than Clyde's men—finding Jack on shore and rescuing him. He wondered what he would do if he ever returned to civilization. Go back to wandering the streets of Florida? Go back to hunting for scraps of food and picking up odd jobs here and there?

Jack frowned and quickly shot to his feet. He narrowed his eyes at the ocean. Turning his back on the vast blue sea, he made a beeline for the edge of the foliage, only stopping when he reached a particularly shady spot to do his exercises. He hated the ocean. He hated it with a passion. Yet for some reason he never had much luck staying away from it.

Jack laughed wryly and began his push-ups. He set his jaw as his arms automatically groaned underneath the weight of his body. He had never been small, necessarily, but more along the lines of solid. Only after a few years on the streets and plenty of time on a Godforsaken island did he feel the corded muscles rippling across his back. He had never felt the need to be physically fit, but now it gave him something to do—something to accomplish. Plus, he worked up an appetite for the bland meals he had quickly grown to despise. Exercise was good for some things, at least.

Twenty minutes later, after multiple reps of multiple exercises, Jack did a few light stretches to loosen up. The sun was going to set in five hours, he knew, and he still had fruit to pick.

Opting to take the longer route to the fruit trees, Jack crossed over the beach and steeled himself against the sizzling sun. His footsteps sank in the wavy sand. He quickened his pace for the fruit grove.

Chapter 8

P RESENT DAY

There was nothing Hayley wanted more than to ditch school and be on spring break already. Actually, there was something she wanted more—to find out what Gran was "researching"—but school was so emotionally and mentally draining that she couldn't function enough to work at her after-school job properly.

Hayley was a waitress at the Coco's restaurant a few blocks from her apartment. She worked six days a week and earned a fair amount of pay, enough to buy herself groceries, clothing, and other necessities. Her parents paid her rent, though she hadn't talked to them since Christmas. They weren't exactly on speaking terms, which was why Hayley took comfort in living close to her grandmother.

After wiping down her last table and heading to the bathroom to change out of her work clothes, Hayley headed home to her apartment. She was beyond tired, so when her phone suddenly came to life with its ringtone, she answered it reluctantly.

"Honey, I've got some big news." Of course it was Gran, who else would be calling her at this time of night?

"Why are you still awake?" Hayley asked groggily.

"I took a nap earlier. I'm so excited to tell you the news."

"I'll bite. What news?"

"Are you on your way home from work?"

"Yes."

"Stop by my place and I'll tell you." It was hard not to miss the excitement in Gran's voice. "See you in a few, sweetheart."

"Hang on, what are you—?" Hayley groaned when she got cut off when Gran ended the call. "After all these years, she still has the nerve," she grumbled, shoving her phone back into her purse. Her neck felt oddly naked without a camera strap hanging from it. She made a mental note to stop by her apartment first before going to Gran's. The surprise can wait, she told herself.

Once she reached her apartment complex, she unlocked her front door and strode inside. She dropped her work clothes on the kitchen table, trading them for her camera. As soon as she swung the strap around her neck, she felt much better and resumed her walk to Gran's.

"Alright, spill," she said when she pushed open the door to Gran's apartment.

Gran smiled. She had been pacing back and forth in the living room, the same travel magazine in her hand from yesterday. She held it out for her granddaughter to see. "Take a look."

Hayley stretched out her tan fingers. Her gaze flitted over Gran's face. Obviously, Gran was worked up about something—maybe she was planning a vacation?—and Hayley's curiosity was at its max. She snatched the magazine and didn't even bother to sit down as she flipped through the pages.

"124," Gran said, pointing to one of the dog-eared corners.

Hayley obediently flipped to the appropriate page. She drank in every word the magazine said—something about a boat adventure through the Florida Keys. Her excited smile, lit up by curiosity, slowly dissolved into a puzzled frown. "What's this?" she asked, finally tearing her gaze off the page to look at Gran.

"It's what I've been researching," she said, breathless with anticipation. "Just look." She pointed with a gnarled finger at headline: Queen Floridian Boat Tours. "It would only be for one week, with daily stops along various islands, and all the sun and sea you could imagine. It's perfect!"

"I don't think I'm following you." Hayley chewed on her bottom lip, confused. "Why on earth would you want to take a boat trip, Gran? I thought you used to get horribly seasick."

"It's not for me, honey." Gran laughed lightly and jabbed another finger at the magazine. "I researched this for you."

Hayley narrowed her eyes. The pieces immediately fell into place, and she violently shook her head. "I have college, remember? There's no way I'm taking a weeklong boat trip to who knows where. That's ridiculous. Plus, there's my job, homework, studying—"

"When is spring break?" Gran asked, the corners of her lips turning up into a knowing smile.

Hayley realized she was stuck. She folded her arms across her chest. "No."

"Honey, this is the perfect opportunity for you. I have everything figured out. I can pay for the cost. All you have to do is pack your things and step on that boat. It would be a wonderful break from college and work."

"I don't need a break," Hayley argued. Okay, so maybe she was looking forward to a break from her college classes. And she wasn't exactly the biggest fan of working night shifts at Coco's. Gran seemed to know this as well, and one look at her grandmother made Hayley sink to the couch in defeat.

"Why do you want me to go so badly?" she asked.

"It would be an adventure," Gran gushed. "You're too much of a homebody. When's the last time you went on an adventure?"

"When I took you to Costco," Hayley muttered.

"When was the last time you went on a vacation? When have you gone a trip to get away from everything? When did you ever take time to relax and let yourself—"

"Okay!" Hayley leaned her head back and groaned in frustration. "I get it. You want me to go have fun over spring break. Can't I just do that from my apartment? I don't need some rugged boat trip to have an adventure."

Gran nodded. "You don't. But that would make one heck of a portfolio, wouldn't it?"

Hayley almost laughed out loud at her typically soft-spoken grandmother. She fingered the camera dangling around her neck, tracing her fingertips over the lens. "Why are you so adamant about this?" she finally asked.

Gran lowered herself onto the couch next to Hayley. She took the magazine from her hand and held it close. "I'm doing this for your sake. Trust me when I say that every college student needs an adventure."

"What if I'm part of the minority who doesn't?"

"Trust me," Gran repeated with a loving smile. "It's not healthy to do the same thing day after day. You need to get away from the world for a little while. No homework, no studying, no working—just the warm sun, refreshing water, and blue horizon stretching as far as the eye could see."

Hayley cracked a smile. "Yep, you've definitely been doing some research," she said, causing Gran to laugh. "You really know how to paint a picture with your words."

"It's more than just a picture, honey. This is a much-needed vacation that you are going to go on next week." She lightly tapped her granddaughter's chest.

Hayley sighed. "I don't know. It sounds fun and all, but it's not really my thing."

"Adventures usually aren't."

"I don't desire an adventure, Gran. It doesn't really appeal to me. I appreciate all the time you've spent researching this, but it doesn't interest me at all. I don't think I can do this." Hayley yawned and slowly got to her feet. "I really need to get some sleep."

Gran smiled sadly and placed the travel magazine onto the coffee table. She walked Hayley to the front door and placed a leathery hand on her shoulder. "Just remember," she said, "a girl has to step out of her comfort zone every once in a while."

Hayley nodded politely and wished her grandmother goodnight. Whatever had possessed Gran to get such ideas in her head, Hayley hoped it would go away by the time spring break rolled around. If there was one person in this entire apartment complex who was least likely to go on an "adventure," it was Hayley. She could envisage her own grandmother taking a boat trip on the wild seas at eighty years old. Hayley simply wasn't cut out for those types of things.

She collapsed on her bed without another thought. Sleep quickly took over.

Chapter 9

"I'm making a huge mistake," Hayley muttered as she sat on her bed, her bulging suitcase lying open in front of her. "This is going to be a disastrous trip." She sighed and rested her head in her hands, wondering why on earth she had let Gran convince her into taking this vacation. In the end, though, she knew she had no one to blame except herself. The adventurous side of her—small though it was—had made refusal impossible. She didn't have to go to class or work for an entire week. The Caribbean would prove to be a beautifully photogenic place. It seemed like a wonderful boat trip.

But the paranoid side of Hayley thought the opposite. What if there's a storm? What if I get seasick? What if the boat starts sinking and we get lost in the middle of the ocean?

Suddenly, Hayley's ringtone startled her out of her thoughts. She picked it up and frowned when she didn't recognize the number.

"Hello?" she asked tentatively, deciding if the caller was some serial killer who had been stalking her for the past ten years, she would be in the middle of the Caribbean by sunset tomorrow night anyway.

"Hi Hayley! It's Oliver."

She breathed a sigh of relief. "Oh, hey. What's up?"

"Um, j-just wondering how your first day of spring break is going."

"Good. How's yours?" Hayley glanced down at her wrist-watch. She only had thirty minutes until she had to be at the dock.

"Fine. I'm doing good."

"Hey, you never texted me about that math test. I'm guessing you found someone to help you...?"

"Oh, y-yeah," he stammered. "I did okay. It wasn't that hard."

"Good. So, Oliver, I kind of have to get going...I'm leaving on a trip and my boat leaves in half an hour."

"Oh! Okay. Are you c-coming back?"

Hayley couldn't help but smile. "Yes, I'm coming back. I'll be back the day before school starts again."

"Right. Um, have fun, Hayley."

She laughed softly. "Bye, Oliver." She pictured his goofy smile and friendly eyes when he bid her goodbye. With one last sigh, she shoved her phone into her pocket and zipped her suitcase closed. She glanced warily at the ticket lying on her bed. There's still time to back out. I don't have to go.

She frowned and buried her head in her hands. Indecision was tearing her apart. She had thought this boat trip ridiculous from the very beginning, but at the same time it lured her in with a forbidden thrill. Remembering Gran's words, Hayley stood up and gathered her belongings. Maybe if I'm lucky, this will only be a small adventure. Nothing too serious.

Hayley stuffed her ticket into her pocket and headed out the door. With each step, she felt a surge of confidence. Though she was still worried, she was also anticipating the beautiful snapshots she would come home with. "I hope you're right, Gran," she murmured as she turned off all the lights in her apartment. She gave her keys to Gran and said goodbye. They embraced with hopeful smiles on both their faces.

"Enjoy yourself," the elderly lady said. "But not too much."

Hayley laughed. "I'll try my best."

Her heart was pounding in her chest by the time she rushed down to the taxi and sped off towards the sea. Once she reached the harbor, she paid the taxi driver her fee and hopped out. Her suitcase felt a little lighter as she drank in the refreshing sea breeze. She took in the beautiful white sand fringed by the cerulean tide. Mangroves overshadowed the wooden dock. On the far side of the harbor she spotted a patch of light blue water. Small waves appeared out of nowhere to lap at the vibrant coral heads growing underneath.

And then Hayley saw it—The Queen Francis. Its size was in between that of a yacht and a cruise ship, with various striped hues running across its hull. Hayley immediately felt relaxed. There was no way a boat that size could capsize in a fluke storm. Gran had been right; this mini vacation was practically harmless.

Hayley grinned and quickened her pace towards the boat. She edged by various people milling about the harbor. After waiting in line to board The Queen Francis, she checked in and was given directions to her room. It was slightly smaller than the size of a normal bedroom, with a twin bed, chair, and small dresser. Hayley immediately began unpacking, already feeling significantly better about the situation.

Once she felt at home in her temporary bedroom, she decided to head back up to the deck and get one last view of the harbor. She had no intentions of mingling with the other passengers, but halfway up the stairs she was obliged to say hello to four different people. Her heart swelled with excitement. This isn't bad. This isn't bad at all.

She strolled across the deck and propped her elbows up on the railing. Though the sun was scorching, causing her tank top to stick to her sweaty back, the cool sea breeze drifting in from the ocean was refreshingly pleasant. She closed her eyes and took out a deep breath, then let it out slowly. She listened to the squawking of seagulls and murmuring of passengers before a sudden conversation jerked her attention.

She frowned and glanced over her shoulder. The wind, which had picked up slightly, blew a few tendrils of her brown hair in front of her eyes. She quickly swept them away and watched curiously as a handful of men noisily boarded the boat. She wondered if they were coworkers on a vacation or simply old friends spending time together. The glint in each of their eyes said otherwise, however.

Hayley immediately felt her skin prickling with goosebumps. Something in those men's expressions gave the impression they were up to no good. Some wore dirty T-shirts and others had rolled up their long sleeves to their elbows, showing hard and corded muscle. Hayley's eyes widened when one of the men caught her staring. To her relief, he gave an easy smile before disappearing to the lower level.

She let out a breath she hadn't even known she was holding in. She laughed softly. To think that she was worried about a strange-looking group of men—now that was ridiculous. She was going to have a good time on The Queen Francis. There was nothing to worry about. This vacation was going to be as relaxing and enjoyable as Gran promised.

Chapter 10

Hayley's first night aboard The Queen Francis proved rather uneventful. After she dined with the other passengers and took a few pictures of the sunset glinting off the calm Caribbean water, she settled into her room. It only took a few minutes to get dressed and ready for bed. She lay awake a while, listening to the rocking of the boat and trying not to concentrate on seasickness. She had heard a few passengers vomiting earlier and thanked God she wasn't as prone to seasickness as they were.

The next morning, Hayley awoke to a golden dawn.

She was up just after sunrise and strolled along the deck, making polite conversation with a few people. During breakfast, the captain made an appearance and announced they would be arriving at the first stop this afternoon. Hayley was delighted.

She hadn't known she would be island-hopping on this exotic adventure. As soon as the first glimpse of land appeared on the horizon, she grabbed her camera and was ready to head ashore.

The Queen Francis docked on the fringe of the coral reef surrounding the island. Through the grapevine, Hayley had found out her boat trip was more of a tour. She and the other passengers would be stopping at a different island each day. All were remote and uninhabited, but safe to explore. Most were less than a quarter-mile in diameter, with a few plants and lots of sand.

Lots of sand.

Hayley and a handful of passengers were rowed to the islands in groups. Once there, they had a few hours to relax and splash in the warm water, or return to The Queen Francis if they wished. Hayley spent as much time as she could off the boat—not because she didn't like it, but because she didn't want to risk getting cabin fever. She soon realized she wasn't a fan of tight spaces. Instead, she relished in the hot Caribbean sun and rolling up her capris to wade in the ocean. She took so many pictures she lost count—some of palm trees, some of the passengers reclining on the beach, and some of the regal boat shimmering in the afternoon sun. Before long, her even tan darkened and she found the courage to wear a bikini in public.

Three days into her journey, Hayley found herself yawning as she retreated down the hallway to her cabin. The sun had gone down an hour ago, and she was already exhausted from the days' events. There was only so much sun and salt she could handle.

Suddenly, a quiet pitter-pattering of footsteps made her pause in her tracks. She whirled around, feeling a chill run down her spine. There hadn't been anyone behind her when she walked down the hallway.

She narrowed her eyes. No one was there. My mind's playing tricks on me, she mused, shaking her head to clear her thoughts. I'm fatigued. Sun-tired. I just need some sleep.

But the same thing happened the next night—except this time, Hayley was mounting the stairs to the deck. She felt the cool wind tousle her hair, which had been uncharacteristically let down rather than pinned up in a bun. Once again, she whirled around upon hearing footsteps, only to realize that no one was there.

This time, though, she didn't blame it on her fatigue.

Hayley let out a shaky breath and rushed onto the deck. She immediately made her way over to a small group of passengers near the railing. She figured if someone was following her, she would have more strength in numbers.

Her heart rate slowed. She gazed over the gunwale at the dark water glinting in the moonlight. A sudden laugh escaped her lips. Strength in numbers? What am I thinking—that someone is going to attack me? The thought was preposterous. But the threat was still there.

Hayley yawned and let the gentle rocking of the boat lure her thoughts away. She pictured Gran's gentle features in her mind's eye. "Every college student needs an adventure," she said.

With a jolt, Hayley realized she had been standing at the railing for over ten minutes. The group next to her had walked away. She was one of the few left on the deck. Rubbing her eyes sleepily, she headed back towards the stairs to return to her cabin.

Murmuring voices grabbed her attention a few moments later. She paused at the top of the stairs and glanced to her side. She suddenly felt slightly more awake than she did seconds ago. She peeked around a few piles of stacked crates. Her eyes immediately bugged out at the sight of the captain.

He had introduced himself as Captain Wooster on her first day aboard The Queen Francis. His easy features and smooth manner of talking had labeled him as a friend right away. No matter how much stress he might be under, he always found time to talk to the other passengers.

Now, though, Hayley had a feeling this wasn't just a typical conversation. She squinted through the darkness at the two men conversing in hushed whispers. Shadows cast behind the crates made their faces barely distinguishable, but she was certain the other man was from the rowdy group she had seen on the day they left the harbor. He was wearing the same dirty T-shirt and soiled shoes, and the expression on his face was even more unpleasant than before.

Hayley swallowed. She couldn't pick out what the men were saying, but her heart thudded in her chest when Captain Wooster suddenly straightened up and placed his hands on his hips. "I'm on a tight schedule," he said, just barely distinguishable to Hayley's ears.

The other man whispered for a few seconds. The Captain leaned forward and held out a hand. Hayley watched curiously as something was passed between the two. The Captain shoved something into the waistband of his pants and tipped his hat to the passenger. Then they parted ways.

Hayley dashed down the stairs. She tried to regulate her breathing in case she met someone in the hallway, but her thoughts were running wild. She darted into her room and locked the door. She wasn't scared that she might have been caught eavesdropping; no, she was certain no one had spotted her.

She was frightened because the Captain had been bribed.

After a fitful sleep, Hayley awoke the next morning with vague memories of her dreams—something about a shipwreck, finding Gran had spontaneously set sail on Hayley's same boat, and seeing two leering faces staring at her through a patch of fog.

Hayley shuddered and quickly changed into her beach attire. She hoped her daily excursion on a remote island would chase away the memory of the bribe. It was alarming to think about. Why would someone bribe Captain Wooster? What plan did those surly men have up their sleeves? Whatever it was, they were up to no good. That much was clear.

With her camera hanging from her neck, Hayley chowed her way through two pieces of toast and a small fruit salad in the dining cabin. For just eight in the morning, the sun was already hot and merciless. It was going to be a steamy one today.

Hayley dawdled about the dining cabin and deck for the next few hours, wondering when The Queen Francis would drop anchor. She snapped a few pictures of various islands she saw on the horizon. The Caribbean seemed to be littered with them. Apparently Captain Wooster had his sights set somewhere else.

It was one in the afternoon when the announcement was finally made. They were to drop anchor in twenty minutes. The captain apologized for the delay in reaching the island, but he promised this one would be much larger than the rest. "It's extremely important that we stay as a group," he said. "You must not leave the designated beach where we will row ashore."

Hayley slathered on sunscreen and waited anxiously on deck. She watched their destination grow larger and larger on the horizon as The Queen Francis glided forward. As she paced back and forth near the railing, two crew members drifted past her, talking in quiet volumes.

"I don't get it either," one said. "We've never gone off course before."

"The Cap'n knows what he's doing. We'll be gone before nightfall. He said so."

"I don't doubt that. I'm just a little surprised by the whole situation. What would make Wooster suddenly go to an island he's never visited before? It's all shady to me. I don't..."

Their voices dipped out of earshot as the men rounded the corner, leaving Hayley standing alone, stunned. She couldn't believe what she had just heard. So the crew had no idea we were coming here? That's odd.

She shivered despite the glaring sun. Though the crew was obviously puzzled, things were slowly starting to add up in Hayley's mind. Captain Wooster can't be in the wrong. He must have a reason for this random excursion. That reason, she predicted, had to have something to do with the bribe.

Suddenly, leaving the safety of The Queen Francis for a strange—and larger—new island seemed slightly risky. But Hayley didn't have much time to ponder this strange turn of events, as a man's voice rang above the excited chatter of the passengers on deck.

"Land ho!"

Chapter 11

There was a flurry of excitement on deck. Passengers ooh'd and ahh'd at the magnificent island in front of them. It was certainly larger than the previous isles, but this one also had a mysterious air about it. The shimmering golden bay, fringed by white sand, tapered off into a lush jungle that swallowed up the rest of the island. Hayley couldn't make out anything else other than towering cliffs in the background.

No sooner than The Queen Francis anchored, passengers were already cramming into the rowboats to go ashore. Everyone was given directions not to wander off. Hayley snorted. *Yeah, not like it's the company's problem if someone gets lost. We all signed emergency waivers.*

Squinting against the glare of the sun, Hayley waited her turn in line until there was a vacant rowboat. She squeezed in next to a tanned young couple and fingered her camera strap anxiously. She watched The Queen Francis grow smaller and smaller while the island grew closer and closer. Still, the only things she could make out were dense foliage and large cliffs. The jungle looked especially dark and forbidding close-up. *Why did we come here?* she wondered.

Fortunately, her spirits brightened once she set foot on the sandy, white shore. She blinked and looked at her surroundings like someone long accustomed to seeing deserted islands. She realized, with a sudden hint of embarrassment, that though this island was bigger, it was just like all the rest.

Hayley fell into her routine of sunbathing, taking pictures, and wading in the cool water. A group of teenagers wandered near the jungle, but they were quickly called back by one of the crew members who patrolled the shore. Hayley was so caught up in watching them that she didn't see another group slinking into the jungle behind her. At least, she didn't until she heard a stifled cough. She whirled around, surprised. She thought she'd been sitting farther down the beach than anyone else. She preferred solitude, after all.

She narrowed her eyes. There was no one there. "Great," she muttered. "My mind's playing tricks on me again." She remembered distinctly the times she had heard footsteps on the boat. She was a little nervous about the idea of someone following her. Was someone still trying to sneak up on her, even on an island in broad daylight?

Hayley gasped and shot to her feet. She got a glimpse of three—no, four—shadows moving through the dark foliage of the jungle. So someone was out there. And by the looks of things, it was probably that surly group of men.

Hayley pulled on her shirt and shorts but left her towel. She made sure her camera was on and ready in one hand. I knew they were trouble. A single picture can prove that once and for all.

If the men were going for a bathroom break—which was a horribly disgusting thought—then Hayley was overreacting about nothing. But if they were doing something dangerous, maybe even something illegal, then she was totally underestimating the situation.

With one fleeting look over her shoulder, Hayley made her decision. She broke out into a jog towards the foliage. Stupid! Stupid, stupid, stupid, her mind chanted, chastising herself for her rash decision. Her cheeks flamed, but she pushed forward anyway. Just one picture, she told herself. She could alert the crew later. The men would be too far away by the time she turned around, convinced the crew what she had seen, and got help. The escapees would be long gone to who-knows-where doing who-knows-what by then.

Hayley picked up her pace. She wasn't even breaking a sweat despite the thick, humid air. The dense brush and jagged roots on the jungle floor forced her to slow down. She swept her gaze from side to side, but the men were nowhere to be seen. All she knew was that they had gone in this direction. I think.

She glanced over her shoulder and groaned. Now the beach was no longer in sight either. She had broken an occasional branch here and there to leave a trail for herself, but it was still scary to be left in the middle of a humid jungle on a deserted island.

Snap.

Or not-so-deserted island.

Hayley's eyes widened. She jumped into a fighting stance, still holding her camera. She waited for a few tense minutes, but she heard nothing else besides the buzzing of mosquitoes. Not even the glimpse of a man's shadow graced her vision.

I'm officially crazy, she decided, rolling her eyes at her own impulsiveness. Might as well go back to the beach before I get myself lost.

Hayley let out a sigh and started walking. Her senses were still on high alert, however. It took all her willpower not to flinch when she heard something snap a few yards behind her. Keep walking. Her heart pounded like an incessant drumline.

She closed her eyes. On the count of three. She ticked off the numbers in her head, then whirled around and broke out into another fighting stance. Unlike her plan, however, it wasn't her pursuer who had been caught off guard—it was herself.

A face, half-hidden by one of the fronds of a dwarf palm, stared at her through the foliage.

A human face.

Chapter 12

Jack hummed to himself as he strolled along the fruit groves. His arms were already laden with oranges and some other tropical fruit he had yet to identify—maybe papaya? It was time to head back to his camp.

He wound his way around large palm trees and short undergrowth until he reached the outer skirmish of the jungle. It was easier to walk along the outskirts than it was through the center of the mosquito-infested foliage. He shifted his load of fruit and carefully stepped over a large pile of driftwood.

Then he froze. He gasped and threw his arms in the air, causing all his fruit to come tumbling onto the sand. He didn't bend down to pick them up, however. He was too busy staring at the ship coming straight towards his island.

It's him, he thought, narrowing his eyes.

But it wasn't. As the ship grew closer, Jack could tell it was much bigger than the boat Clyde and his men had used. He hadn't seen those goons for months. Had Clyde come back with more of his lackeys this time?

Jack didn't want to stick around to find out. Leaving his fruit lying abandoned in the sand, ready to rot, he dashed into the jungle and made a beeline for the cliffs. Even though he had been on the island for six months, he hadn't gotten farther than a hundred yards up the steep cliff face. It was a natural barrier keeping him from exploring the rest of the island.

After a long, sweaty climb, Jack perched himself on a ledge and stared above the leafy jungle. The heat was sweltering. He watched in silent fascination as a few smaller boats—rowboats, apparently—broke away from the larger one. How many people are on this thing? he wondered. And, more importantly, why are they here?

Jack knew the only logical place to land was in the bay. That was where he did his daily swimming in the ocean, and that was where he walked the beach. The rest of the island was fringed by a large reef too shallow for boats to drop anchor.

But what was this boat doing here? Jack's privacy was being intruded, but it didn't look like Clyde was involved. Jack figured it was mere tourists. He knew there were plenty of boats cruising the Caribbean, some for fishing, some for research, some for exploring, and some for travel. He decided the large boat anchored outside the reef was a combination of the latter two. Why else would there be a bunch of random people swarming his beach and reclining on the sand?

He frowned. The whole situation was odd—extremely odd. And here he was, sitting a safe distance away from the one thing he had been waiting six months to find.

Rescue.

With a stab of realization, Jack closed his eyes and banged his head against the rock behind him. "I don't want to be rescued," he muttered. "Why don't I want to be rescued?"

He was frustrated with himself. He knew he should go back to the bay and tell the people he had been marooned. However, deep down, he didn't want to be labeled as a castaway. He had spent the last decade of his life being afraid, and the last few years after that running away from his fears. He had finally found a place where he didn't have to worry about being found (other than by Clyde, of course).

And who was to say Jack couldn't hide from Clyde as well? The next time that brute and his men set foot on the island, Jack could run to the cliffs and stay there until they left. He could make another camp and stock it with provisions for safety measures. After all, if he was still on the island when hurricane season hit, he would be in big trouble if he didn't have a backup shelter.

Jack had made up his mind: he was staying. He brushed the dirt off his raggedy jeans and began climbing down. The tourists off in the distance didn't seem to be moving beyond the beach, which was fine with Jack. This way, he could go back to his camp in the jungle, remove any evidence of himself being there (in case some loony did wander away from the beach), and hightail it back to the cliffs.

But Jack's plan wasn't foolproof. He didn't even make it to Step One before he ran into trouble. Halfway to his camp, he froze when he heard voices murmuring in the jungle a few yards away.

Crap. He crouched low and peered through the leaves of a dwarf palm. His heart immediately began pounding in his chest. *No! This can't be happening. I'm too late.*

Clyde was here. And by the looks of things, he had his Spaniard and a few other wingmen with him as well. This was not looking good.

Jack closed his eyes and forced himself to remain calm. He sorted out the facts in his mind: *Clyde and his men were on that boat, but the other passengers are staying on the beach. Maybe none of the passengers are looking for me. In that case, he only had to worry about Clyde's group.*

And that left Jack with...no plan. He groaned and peeked through the fronds once more. Clyde and his men were moving on in another direction, apparently. Jack breathed a sigh of relief. He might still have time to reach his camp and go back to the cliffs without being found.

The murmuring voices suddenly grew louder. Jack froze again and whirled around. Staying safe in the shadow of a large tree, he watched as Clyde and three other men split up. His gut clenched. *Great. Now I have to avoid them individually instead of just one big group!*

He slowly moved behind the tree and waited until the jungle grew quiet again. The buzz of mosquitoes filled the empty void where Clyde's voice used to be. Jack heard the rustling of bushes off to his left, but other than that, the jungle seemed to be as quiet as always. *If only it could be as harmless, too.*

An invisible threat seemed to hang over Jack's head as he sprinted for his camp. He glanced over his shoulder every now and then, hoping that no one was following him and wishing he knew how to better cover his tracks. Oh well. Clyde already knew he was somewhere on the island; the better question was how long would Clyde search until he found Jack?

Suddenly, for the fourth time that day, Jack gasped and stopped in his tracks. He nearly crashed into a giant root sticking out of the path as he darted behind another tree. Oh no. This is not good. Not good at all.

Jack's head swam with all that had happened in the past thirty minutes. He peeked through the fronds of another dwarf palm and watched the tall, slender girl wandering through the jungle. She seemed to be looking for someone by the way her head constantly turned left and right. Though her back was to him, Jack felt an odd sense of realization dawn on him as he stared at her. She was familiar; so familiar. That brown hair...those toned arms and legs...

The girl suddenly whirled around. Jack flinched, hoping she hadn't heard him. Was it possible she could hear the way his heart was thundering through his ribcage? Whatever the reason, the girl suddenly blanched when her eyes connected with Jack's.

He gasped. It was her.

She screamed.

Chapter 13

Oliver closed his eyes and forced himself to take slow, calming breaths. His fingers were shaking as he slowly stepped up to the deck. The sun nearly blinded him. His hand instinctively flew up to cover his eyes. Ow.

He stumbled towards the railing and waited until his eyes grew adjusted to the brightness. He watched as smiling, chatting passengers were rowed away from The Queen Francis towards the island. *Am I really about to do this?*

He swallowed nervously and took a cautious step backwards. The easiest thing for him to do would be to turn around and go right back to his cabin. He wouldn't show his face until the passengers gathered in the dining cabin for dinner. Or he could take the courageous route and stick to his plan.

Follow Hayley.

"Easier said than done," he muttered to himself. Though this wasn't the first time he had been on a boat, this was the farthest he had ever been from home. He wasn't exactly a fan of traveling. But as soon as Hayley had said she was going on a boat trip, he felt horrible for not saying what he should have said right then and there.

Oliver squeezed his eyes shut and forced the memory away. *What's done is done. I'm just a stuttering fool in Hayley's eyes. I shouldn't have rushed down to the harbor and watched her board this boat. I shouldn't have followed her.* But his instincts had been too much handle. He was a lonely college student with no friends and a family that lived hundreds of miles away in Maine. *I should have known I never had a chance with her.*

Now, watching Hayley's glossy brown hair whip around her shoulders as she glided across the open sea, he felt a sudden surge of bravery. He still had a chance. This wasn't over yet. He just had to get on a rowboat and follow her to that island.

"I'm gonna die," he squeaked, slowly edging towards the line of passengers boarding the remaining rowboats. He must have looked pale and clammy, because when one of the crew helped him off the boat, he grabbed Oliver's arm and asked, "Sir, are you alright?"

Oliver managed a quick nod, but it didn't seem to convince the sailor. Oliver was given a wary look and a polite nudge into the rowboat.

The trip to the island seemed to take hours. Every bump and rough patch of water made Oliver want to heave. He had spent most of his time on The Queen Francis in the head, vomiting or worrying about his poor planning. He hadn't even brought even clothes to last the entire trip—only two shirts, one pair of shorts, some Airwalks and a junky sweatshirt.

Oliver wished, more than anything at that moment, to back in his dorm room. It was an adventure going to Florida for college by himself, for Pete's sake. But now he was on a tourist boat in the middle of the Caribbean chasing a girl who didn't even know he was following her? It was absurd.

"Sir?"

Oliver snapped back to reality. He realized another of the crew was tugging on his sleeve, waiting to help him out of the rowboat. "Sir, we've reached the island. Would you mind stepping out, or do you want to return to the boat?"

Oliver licked his chapped lips and mumbled a few words of apology. He stumbled out of the rowboat, nearly face-planting into the sand in the process. He gathered his wits and swept the shore for any sign of Hayley.

She had a good fifteen-minute start ahead of him, but it looked like she had settled in just fine on her own little section of the beach. Oliver sullenly plopped down in the sand and forced himself not to make eye contact. He suddenly realized he had no plan other than to follow Hayley to the island. Great. Just great.

He sighed and waited patiently. For the next half-hour, he watched and waited and felt himself getting more and more sunburnt. Tourists splashed in the warm water. Oliver sneaked a glance at Hayley in his peripheral vision and saw her taking pictures. People laughed and talked as they built sandcastles on the shore. Hayley had moved back to her towel and was sunbathing. Others were sunbathing now too. Oliver realized his sunburn was getting worse—and he felt an awful lot like a stalker. This wasn't the first time he had followed Hayley without her knowing. He had snuck up behind her on many occasions, but never actually worked up the courage to give away he was on the same boat. What an awkward confrontation that would be—and Oliver was already plenty awkward to begin with. Now he could add Ultimate Stalker Status to his list of faults.

He frowned and let out another sigh. Well, at least I've accomplished something today: I've set foot on my first deserted island.

Yes, this was the first island Oliver had visited, and so far it wasn't living up to his expectations. But then again, what did he expect? Carnivorous plants and shrieking monkeys chucking coconuts from palm trees? Maybe the better question was what he didn't expect—which included happy-go-lucky tourists splashing in the water and tromping all over the beach. They kind of took out the "deserted" in "deserted island."

He sighed for a third time and lay back down in the sand. The hot sun was burning his skin to a crisp, but he didn't mind. His fair skin could use a little tan anyway. Or sunburn. Whichever came first.

Before long, his eyelids drooped closed and he drifted off into a quiet nap. He didn't awake until a few hours later, when the loud chattering of teenagers jolted him out of his sleep. He sat up and rubbed his eyes, puzzled at his surroundings for a few seconds. Then he remembered.

"Oh." He yawned and scratched his head. His glasses were perched crookedly on his nose, so he righted them and sat up straight to keep them from slipping down any further. He suddenly remembered what he was doing and why he was here.

Hayley. He sneaked another glance in her direction, hoping she hadn't strolled along the beach and seen him without Oliver knowing. Then he gasped. Crap! She's gone!

He leaped to his feet. An older gentleman reading a magazine glanced up at him. "Hey, you were blocking the sun for me. Can you sit back down?"

"N-no. Sorry," Oliver stammered, too flustered to give a decent reply. He sped off towards the place where Hayley had been sitting. Her towel was still there, but her clothes were gone. Wherever she went, it's not the water, he mused. He swept his gaze over the beach just to make sure he wasn't overreacting.

She definitely wasn't on the beach. So where is she? Oliver had heard the captain give specific instructions not to leave the area. She has to be here. She has to.

After a few minutes of searching, it was clear where Hayley wasn't—the beach.

That left only two options—the ocean or the jungle. Oliver knew for a fact she wasn't in the water. With a prickly feeling, he turned towards the jungle and swallowed. Hayley, I hope you're not in there...

For all Oliver knew, there could be a hidden spring filled with deadly piranhas or giant Venus flytraps just waiting to devour any person within their reach. He gasped and quickly shook those thoughts from his mind.

Suddenly, a voice rang out above the hordes of passengers swarming the beach. "Attention! Please gather your belongings and return to the rowboats. Everyone needs to leave the shore within the next fifteen minutes. Pick up any trash as well."

Oliver's heart sank. No. No, no, no! He took one more furtive glance towards the jungle before scurrying away. He found Hayley's belongings and stared intently at her towel, which was lying exactly where she had left it. If there was a moment where Oliver wished someone could appear out of thin air, this was it.

"Come on, Hayley," he muttered. "Where are you?" He grew anxious as more and more passengers were loaded into the rowboats. Everyone was leaving. Towels were lifted off the sand. Food wrappers and Coke cans were picked up by the crew and stashed into plastic bags to preserve the identity of the island. Before long, the only things remaining on the beach were footprints, sandcastles, and Hayley's towel.

And Oliver.

"Sir! Sir, everyone is leaving. You have to get in the boat." A crew member pointed a finger at Oliver, then at the boat halfway filled with tourists. Some were scowling impatiently and some looked worn-out from lounging in the sun and saltwater all day.

Oliver glanced over his shoulder at the jungle. He gestured towards Hayley's towel. "Uh, I think there's...um..."

"Oh, someone must have left it." The sailor quickly snatched Hayley's towel and draped it over one shoulder. "Don't worry, we'll find out who it belongs to."

Oliver swallowed. "No, that's not...I m-mean..." He closed his eyes and groaned in frustration.

"Sir, you have to come with me to the rowboat," the sailor said impatiently.

Oliver violently shook his head.

"Now," he added.

Oliver frowned. "Y-you don't understand. Someone's in trouble. L-lots of trouble! Her name is—"

The sailor rolled his eyes and helped Oliver to his feet. "Alright, who's in trouble? What's going on?"

Oliver froze when he spotted a shock of brown hair over the sailor's shoulder. He stepped to the side to get a better view. There, in one of the rowboats already headed back to The Queen Francis, was Hayley!

He breathed a sigh of relief, mentally chastising himself for being such a worrywart. "N-nothing," he stuttered.

"Good. Let's head back, then."

Oliver had never been more relieved to set foot on a boat. He eagerly took a seat next an acne-ridden teenager, bracing himself for the bumpy ride back to The Queen Francis. Back to dinner. Back to his normal routine. And, eventually, back to Florida and his college lifestyle.

I'm never taking another boat tour again.

Chapter 14

Hayley quickly shut her mouth, the last traces of her scream echoing through the jungle. All of a sudden, time seemed to freeze, as if nature was considering whether or not Hayley's scream was a threat. A few moments later, insects resumed their buzzing and a gentle breeze started to blow.

On the other side of the clearing, Jack remained startled. He would recognize that face anywhere. Slowly, cautiously, he peeled back a palm frond and crawled into the clearing. He stood up, his 6-foot frame dwarfing Hayley's petite one. He kept his distance while taking in every feature, from her vibrant green eyes to her toned, tan skin.

"Hayley Slade," he said quietly.

She jumped, startled by his voice. She instinctively backed away a few feet, eyes narrowed. "You know me?" she hissed.

"We went to school together." As soon as the words left Jack's tongue, he realized how silly that sounded. School? He hadn't gone to school in years. High school seemed like a thing of the past—a distant past he hardly remembered nor cared to remember. Yet here was the one person he did remember. His cheeks flushed appropriately.

Hayley forced a laugh. "Um, sorry, but I don't remember you." She backed up a couple more feet. "I think I'm going to leave now..."

Jack realized how different he must look. Not only had it been years since he graduated from high school, but he knew his features had been significantly altered from living on a deserted island for six months. His skin had darkened, his muscles had become more developed, and he was proudly sporting a caveman-style beard and raggedy hair. He surprised both himself and Hayley by laughing out loud.

"I look like a freak, don't I?" he asked.

Hayley let her guard drop for a second. "Well, there's that, and the fact that your voice sounds like a record scratch."

He grinned. "Jack Patterson," he said, sticking out a hand.

Hayley glanced over at the dirt-caked fingers and dark, leathery skin. She wracked her memory for a Jack Patterson. The name surprisingly sounded familiar, but she couldn't connect it with the wild face in front of her. Tentatively, she shook his hand, wiping the dirt off on her shorts a few seconds later. "What school did you go to?" she demanded.

"Orange Grove High," he said without missing a beat.

Hayley's eyebrows shot up. So we did go to school together! "Wow. How'd you end up here?"

"It's a long story."

"I bet."

"You still don't remember me, do you?"

"Sorry, but you don't look familiar at all. Your name rings a bell, but I can't remember anything else."

Jack sighed and hung his head. "Um, okay. How about this: picture a kid with blonde hair, blue eyes, and fair skin, about five foot ten."

"That doesn't narrow it down much."

He winced. "Right. Well, you probably don't remember me anyway. I was awkward. Unsocial. Not athletic or sporty in any way."

Hayley raised an eyebrow. That seemed hard to believe, but with time came change.

"You were the exact opposite, I remember," Jack continued. "The girl with the camera and a shy smile. You were pretty popular."

"I guess. It never did me any good. All of my close friends went to college out of state. I'm a loner at FIU."

"Hey, look at me. I've been stranded on this deserted island for six months. Do you think high school prepared me for this?"

Hayley's smile vanished. "Tell me about it," she said. "Your story, I mean. How you got here."

"It's a long story. There were these men who—"

Suddenly, the click of a gun echoed through the jungle. "That's enough, Jack," a deep voice said. Hayley and Jack turned at the sound, their faces going deathly pale as a group of men emerged from the shadows of the underbrush. Hayley immediately recognized them as the troublemaking group who had abandoned the tourists at the beach. Jack recognized them as Clyde and his lackeys.

"Well, well. I see you're quite the ladies' man," Clyde said casually. He stepped directly behind Jack, pressing the barrel of his Glock 19 into Jack's shoulder blade. Jack grunted but made no movement.

Hayley swallowed, the surprise and curiosity sucked out of her. Now all she felt was fear. Fear, and an urgent sense of regret for thinking she could follow those men into the jungle. She was in over her head now.

Clyde's gaze was unnerving. "Don't look so frightened, Kitty," he drawled, giving Hayley a vicious smile. "Go ahead, Sully." He nodded at one of his men, who marched over and grabbed both of Hayley's arms. Sully jerked them behind her back and held them there to make sure there was no chance she could escape—not that there had been much of a chance anyway.

"Bring Cat Eyes over here," Clyde demanded. "And take her camera."

Hayley almost cried out when her precious camera was ripped over her head. She was shoved forward until she was only a few feet away from Jack. Their eyes met for a brief second. Jack's lips were drawn taut and his face had hardened into a look of pure anger.

Clyde stared into Hayley's green orbs. "Mind telling us what you're doing away from the beach, disobeying Cap'n's orders?" he asked.

I could ask the same of you. She forced herself to hold Clyde's gaze and remain silent.

"How do you know Jack here?"

Hayley closed her eyes. *Breathe. Just breathe.* Her heart was racing. She didn't know whether it would be wise or foolish to tell the truth. If she denied knowing Jack, maybe they would let her go. But she was quick to dismiss the thought. Who knew how long the men had surrounded them, overhearing their conversation? And why would they ever let Hayley go? She had too much knowledge, and she figured this little escapade of theirs was supposed to be kept under the radar.

Clyde shoved the Glock harder against Jack's shoulder blade. "If you won't talk, we'll have to do this the hard way," he growled. He grabbed Jack's arm and spun the youth around, giving him a hard left hook that sent Jack stumbling to the ground.

"Stop!" Hayley shrieked, lunging forward. Sully tightened his grip around her arms, and she stumbled as well. "Look, I've never met Jack before. I don't know what you have against him or why you've outmanned us four to two. Do you really think we're going to fight you or run away? Can't we just talk this through?"

The men snickered. Clyde laughed, his spittle landed just a few inches shy of her face. "We're no diplomats, sweetheart. We do this our way. And that means you and Jack are coming with us."

Hayley felt tears spring into her eyes when Sully twisted her arms. She forced herself not to cry out from the pain. "Here's the rules," he hissed into her ear, his foul breath causing her to shiver. "You don't talk, you don't scream, you don't run. If anyone asks you anything, don't speak a word of this, or you'll find a bullet in your head. Got it?"

Hayley nodded fearfully, tears now streaming. She glanced over at Jack, who was slowly pushing himself off the ground.

Clyde grabbed him and whispered fiercely in his ear as well. Oh, no. What have I gotten myself into?

The trek through the jungle was one of the longest walks Hayley had ever experienced. She and Jack were separated by the Spaniard, but every so often she would hear a muffled grunt and know he was still okay. The men talked quietly or cracked a few jokes, as if kidnapping two kids was their normal business. Maybe it was. Hayley had no idea.

To her surprise, when they finally reached the outskirts of the jungle, The Queen Francis was still in plain sight. None of the other boats were in the water, nor were any tourists left on the beach. Hayley wished there was something she could do to alert The Queen Francis for help, but with her arms pinned behind her back and her captors wielding guns, she didn't have any options.

"Where's our boat?" Clyde demanded.

"It should be in this area," one of his lackeys replied.

"Well, find it!"

He darted off, leaving soft footprints in the glittering sand. Hayley and the others were soon sweating underneath the tropical sun. When the man returned ten minutes later with said rowboat, Hayley and Jack were shoved into the aft, followed by Clyde and his other lackeys. With the sun now setting, the water was illuminated in bold colors, but Hayley was much too worried about her and Jack's fates to appreciate the beauty. Their eyes met for a second time, and he mouthed the words, "I'm sorry."

She looked away, knees shaking and palms sweating. Though Jack seemed frustrated and angry, Hayley was panicked. My first boat trip, and I've already been kidnapped. Wait until Gran hears about this. Just the thought of her beloved grandmother brought a second round of tears to her eyes.

The men rowed for about half an hour before resting and letting themselves drift. The island was still large and mysterious, but it wasn't the only object on the horizon. The Queen Francis was slowly making her way toward the rowboat. Hayley was shocked when the two boats finally made contact shortly after sunset. She strained to see through the hazy twilight, but couldn't make out any passengers or crew on the starboard side.

Suddenly, one of the men hoisted Hayley to her feet. As Clyde and the other men climbed onboard The Queen Francis, they pulled Hayley and Jack after them. She grunted in discomfort but didn't call for help. The warning given to her was still clear in her mind. She was also confused about why they were back on the tour boat. What was the point of being kidnapped and held at gunpoint if Clyde just deposited her back on The Queen Francis? Was this part of the bribe with Captain Wooster?

As if reading her thoughts, Clyde grabbed Hayley's and Jack's biceps and pulled them close. "Not a word," he growled. "If either of you so much as breathes a word to the other passengers, you'll get a bullet to the head. If you try to sneak off to an island or jump overboard, you'll get a bullet to the head. If you go anywhere except the dining hall and your quarters, you'll get a bullet to the head."

"I like how you vary things up," Jack quippd.

"Shut up," Clyde warned, narrowing his eyes. "I think you get the picture. Not a word to each other; not a word to the other passengers."

Jack looked amused. Hayley was petrified and shaking from head to toe, wondering how he could appear so casual under the circumstances.

"Take her," Clyde said, finally releasing Hayley to two of his men. They immediately grabbed her arms and hustled her across the deck. Once they descended the stairs, they let go and walked side by side, trying not to draw attention from the other passengers. Hayley put on the most fearful gaze she could muster, but nobody paid her any attention as the men surreptitiously guided her through the shadows.

"Where's your room?" one of them demanded. Hayley feebly told him, and she was escorted directly to her quarters. She was given another warning, then left alone for the night. She quickly closed and locked her door, her hands still shaking. *Thank God they're gone. Now what am I supposed to do?* She couldn't alert Captain Wooster. She had no friends on board. Clyde hadn't hinted what he was going to do with her—maybe he didn't even know himself. It seemed like she had jumped into the middle of a long-lasting quarrel between him and Jack.

Meanwhile, Jack was also "escorted" to a room, but quicker and with much stealth. He had been amused when Clyde told him not to speak to the other passengers. *How was he supposed to blend in when he looked like a castaway?*

Apparently Clyde had already thought that through. After Jack was carefully kept out of sight and forced into a room, he was told to take a shower, shave, and make himself presentable. Even though he detested doing anything Clyde ordered him to do, he couldn't deny that the idea of taking a shower sounded heavenly.

Jack was given a fresh shirt, jeans, and shoes. All three were a little snug, but as soon as he was locked inside the head with a bodyguard right outside the door, he held them close to his face and relished in the smell of clean clothes.

For the next twenty minutes, Jack scrubbed himself raw and shaved until his cheeks seemed to sparkle. The entire time, his mind flitted between Clyde and Hayley. For the life of him, he couldn't figure out why Clyde was on a civilian boat. What was the point in that? Why would Clyde risk putting Jack in a situation where he could possibly escape? He knew Clyde's men would shadow him at every turn, but he was determined to find some way off the boat.

Then there was Hayley. His stomach clenched at the mere thought of her. Talk about a blast from the past! She had been one of the most popular girls at Orange Grove, whereas Jack had been a pasty high school kid, an awkward social pariah. It was obvious why he could remember her and not the other way around. Yet he hoped with all his heart that she would make the connection and remember who he was, even though his past wasn't all that spectacular.

Jack frowned at himself in the mirror. *Who am I kidding? I shouldn't be worrying about whether Hayley remembers me. I need to start thinking of a way out of this.*

Chapter 15

Jack awoke to the murmuring of voices. He slowly pushed himself up with one arm and blinked rapidly in the hazy morning glow. For a moment he wondered what had made the ground in his cave suddenly so soft, but then he remembered.

"Look who's awake," a deep voice said. Three pairs of eyes immediately turned to Jack, who frowned and sat up in his bed.

Clyde, who was seated in in between lackeys, smiled mischievously. "Did you get a good rest, Sleeping Beauty?"

"Best I've had in a while," Jack muttered.

Suddenly, all three men lunged forward. Before Jack even knew what was happening, his arms were pinned to the wall behind him and Clyde had shoved his hands up against Jack's chest. "So, Nau," he spat, "enlighten us. Now that the nosy girl's gone, you can tell us everything we need to know. Starting with the map."

Jack squared his jaw. The confrontation brought back memories of being beaten on another boat shortly before being abandoned on the island. He was a pro at this, but it still didn't keep the nerves away.

"Every second you're quiet is another second we waste looking for that treasure." Clyde shoved Jack harder against the wall, evoking a small grunt.

"I told you before; I don't know."

"That's not good enough."

"Sorry, but that's the way it is. I don't have your stupid map."

Clyde narrowed his eyes. In a split second, he relieved the pressure on Jack's chest and used one hand to slap him in the face. Jack recoiled, his cheek stinging. "You had six months!" Clyde roared. "Why do you think we kept you alive that long, boy?"

Jack remained silent, which proved to aggravate Clyde even more. "Tell me!" he screeched.

"I. Don't. Know."

A backhand slap. Jack's face was flung in the opposite direction. Now both of his cheeks were stinging, and his upper lip was cut diagonally, exposing a portion of his teeth. He swallowed and tasted blood.

Clyde cursed and began pacing across the floor. As he muttered to himself, Jack ran over the options in his head. All three men were unarmed, as far as he could see—unless they were carrying handguns in the backside of their jeans. If he could just break his arms free and launch himself across the room—provided the door was unlocked—he could dash upstairs and alert the Captain. He didn't believe Clyde was telling the truth when he said he would shoot Jack. Jack was precious; the only link to the treasure map. Clyde wouldn't dare kill him.

But he would kill Hayley. Jack shuddered at the thought. He was annoyed at the single major flaw in his plans—Hayley. If it wasn't for her, he could force his way out of this mess. But now that she was involved, he felt obligated to protect her, even if she still didn't remember him from Orange Grove.

"Lock him in the head," Clyde demanded. Jack struggled as the two men easily overpowered him and shut him inside the bathroom. They slammed the door and stuffed furniture on the outside to keep Jack from prying it open.

Jack sighed and plopped down on the floor. He realized that they had cleared the head of all supplies while he had been sleeping. There were no razors, no shaving cream, no tools of any kind to possibly help him or entertain him—or hurt him. To make things worse, Jack's stomach felt like it was folding in on himself, he was so hungry. He hadn't eaten since yesterday afternoon. Would Clyde even allow him to get breakfast?

Chapter 16

After tossing and turning all night, numb with fear and unsure of how to cope with yesterday's events, Hayley finally awoke. Though she was relieved to find none of Clyde's men snooping around her quarters, she showered and dressed with caution. Her stomach growled, but she spent nearly a half hour pondering whether or not to go upstairs to the dining hall. What if one of the bad guys was right outside her door? What if they decided to just shoot her for no reason?

She was nearly driven mad with what-ifs. She finally decided to open her door a few inches, with her entire body weight behind it in case she needed to slam it closed in an emergency. She sucked in her breath and reminded herself not to be too rash. I should only yell for help if I need it, she told herself, or else I'll get a bullet in my head.

She unlocked the door. She pushed it open one inch, then two. An elderly couple sauntered by, but no one else was in sight. Hayley fingered the empty space around her neck where a camera strap should have been. She narrowed her eyes and pushed open her door all the way. The coast was clear.

Nimble and light on her feet, Hayley glided into the hallway and locked her door behind her. After glancing left and right, she headed upstairs to the dining hall. So far so good.

Just as she rounded the corner, her heart leapt into her throat. She froze and had to force herself to keep walking. One of Clyde's men was casually observing the passengers walking to and from the dining hall. When his gaze landed on Hayley, he grinned toothily. It wasn't a friendly smile.

Hayley swallowed and quickened her pace. She let out a sigh of relief when she slipped inside the dining hall, thinking she was out of sight. But when she turned to get in line for food, another one of Clyde's men was directly behind her. She shrieked. A few passengers turned and gave her wary looks, so she ducked her head. Idiot.

"A bit jumpy today, aren't we?" the man whispered down her neck. His breath made Hayley's blood run cold. She ignored him and pressed forward in line. As soon as she piled some breakfast on her plate, she rushed downstairs into her quarters, locking the door behind her. The only sound was the sizzling of bacon and her own heartbeat as she shook with fear.

The rest of the meals went the same. Hayley was sick with fright, eating all of her meals in her quarters and never knowing when Clyde or his lackeys would pounce. They seemed to be everywhere—in the dining hall, on the deck, meandering through the hallways. She had never been so afraid.

Occasionally her thoughts drifted to her Gran, and on more than one occasion she felt tears spring into her eyes.

She missed her dear grandmother and the luxury of feeling safe. She hated The Queen Francis with a passion. Soon, her cabin fever became too much to handle, and Hayley dared to eat dinner in the dining hall instead of cooped up in her quarters. Though she felt eyes on her back, she acted as normal as possible. At least I'm not starving or being held at gunpoint, she thought, which brought Jack to mind. She hadn't seen him once since they had been shown to separate rooms last night. I hope he's okay...

The boat trip had become a nightmare. Another day went by. Hayley was slowly becoming less and less fearful, but her nerves never went away completely. She was bored out of her mind, too, since she was forbidden to go to any of the islands the other passengers visited. And she had still yet to see Jack.

Finally, the following night, Hayley took her usual seat in the dining hall and was shocked to see Jack enter the room a few moments later. Her eyes nearly bugged out of their sockets when she saw his cleanly-shaven face and trimmed hair. A younger face suddenly came to mind. Jack Patterson. She almost smiled in relief when the memory came to her. So that's Jack Patterson!

With his rugged Neanderthal look gone, Jack looked more like his old self. Hayley gaped at the obvious differences between now and high school. He had definitely grown taller and slimmed down. The strong, corded muscles were an evident improvement as well. He was a far cry from the shy, socially awkward student at Orange Grove years ago.

Hayley suddenly realized she had been staring for far too long. She quickly ducked her head and resumed eating. She picked at her food halfheartedly until a napkin suddenly flitted into view. She paused, curious. It looked like someone had accidentally let the napkin slip between their fingers, but when she picked it up and turned it over in her hands, she realized it had been strategically placed with the blank side facing up. On the opposite side was a barely decipherable scrawl.

Her senses automatically went on high alert. She glanced up, knowing full well what the consequences would be if Clyde caught her with this note. Fortunately, his men had their attention directed at Jack, who was bent over a few tables away tying his shoe.

Hayley let out a deep breath and placed the napkin underneath her plate, sliding it forward a few inches so she could read while her arms shielded the napkin from prying eyes.

Hayley, don't do anything rash. Stay out of trouble. Clyde needs to keep me alive, but he has no leverage with you. Tell him you know nothing. Meet me on deck in 15 minutes.

That was all it said. Hayley had to reread a few sentences, since the writing was unbearably small and blotted in multiple places. She cautiously ripped the napkin in half and threw it away with the remains of her dinner. She waltzed around the dining hall for a few minutes, watching the clock until she deemed it was time to leave. Once outside, she paced up and down the deck, trying to appear as normal as possible.

Her breath caught in her throat when she spotted Jack. He was approaching from the stern, his eyes anywhere but on Hayley. He paused at the railing for a few seconds, then turned to leave. Hayley was confused when he disappeared downstairs, two of Clyde's men shadowing him. But then she saw a smattering of white against the dark blue of the railing. She walked as inconspicuously as possible to the stern, her heart hammering in her chest. Once she was at the spot where Jack had stood just moments before, she casually groped underneath the railing until she held three crumpled napkins in her hand.

They had been stuck to the railing by a piece of gum, which Hayley tried to ignore as she stuffed the napkins into her pocket. After gazing dispassionately at the ocean for a few minutes, she headed back to her quarters, eager to read Jack's notes.

She was fairly certain Clyde's men hadn't spotted their rendezvous. But then again, it was extremely hard to tell where they were at times. They could be anywhere from the shadows, watching her, to just an arm's length away. She shuddered and locked the door behind her.

Finally, privacy. She turned the napkins over in her hands. All sides were covered in Jack's trademark scrawl. Hayley wondered when he had found the time to do this. Clyde's men seemed to be shadowing him even more than they did her. Maybe he had snuck into the head and scribbled everything down in secret.

Hayley peered down at the napkins and began to read.

I'm so sorry for involving you in this mess. Though I don't think you remember me, I feel like I have to explain some things to you. Here's a bit of my past: after high school, I spent most of my time avoiding a dangerous crowd of thieves

She flipped the napkin over.

and criminals. I never went to college. I had to stay under the radar. It didn't work out, obviously, and Clyde found me six months ago when I was wandering the streets of Key Largo. His men

Hayley skimmed the remaining two napkins, flipping them over until she found the one that finished the previous sentence.

kidnapped me and forced me onto their boat. I was beaten and threatened. They accused me of having a treasure map. I didn't tell them what they wanted to hear, so they left me on a deserted island, where I'd been living for six months.

To my surprise, Clyde made sure there was no way I could leave the island, but plenty of resources to survive on the island. He wanted me alive but without contact to the world. That's why I'm positive he won't kill me, but he can

The final napkin. Hayley's heart was pounding now.

still kill you. Please don't do anything you'll regret. Don't speak to any of the passengers or crew. In case you're wondering where I am, Clyde's been keeping me in his quarters. They only let me "wander" the ship last night for the first time. But don't worry—I

have a plan. (Sort of.) Just stay out of trouble and don't look so afraid. When I saw you in the dining hall the other day, you looked white as a ghost. Try to cover your tracks a bit. Oh, and Clyde still has your camera. Don't worry; it's completely fine. – Jack

Hayley didn't know whether to be embarrassed that she was such a scaredy-cat or amused that Jack remembered she was a photographer. Of all the things he mentioned, he included her camera. How sweet. She thought it strange, though, that Jack never stated if he had the map Clyde was looking for. He hadn't confirmed it, but he hadn't denied it, either. Hayley felt like he was keeping something from her. I want to trust you, Jack, but there are still things you aren't telling me. We need to find a way to talk face-to-face.

Chapter 17

J ack was running out of time. It was obvious Clyde thought Jack had the map, or at least knew of its whereabouts. That morning Clyde had even suggested Jack purposely destroyed the map and memorized it. Jack had laughed out loud, which had earned him a punch and blow to the stomach that knocked the wind out of him. As he was doubled over, chest heaving, eyes staring at the bleak wooden floor, another one of his incidents hit him. He was suddenly bombarded with light and images. Words flitted across his vision. Nothing was decipherable, however. It all vanished within a second.

Jack groaned and let himself slump to the floor. Why couldn't he remember? He felt pulled to the strange words and images that came with each flash of light. He needed to visualize them once more. He needed to get a good, long look.

"I'm getting tired of this, Nau,"Clyde said, using his favorite nickname for Jack. "My patience is running thin."

"Then kill me."

"You know I can't do that—not unless you show me the map."

"You already have my answer."

"It's the wrong answer!"

Jack shrugged. Clyde grabbed the youth's head kneed him in the stomach. Jack felt like his entire torso had been crushed. He lay in fetal position on the floor, cradling his stomach and moaning. Clyde's men snickered and drew closer to watch the show.

"We can do this all day, or you can spare yourself the pain and spare me precious time. Where is the map?"

Jack squeezed his eyes shut and tried to block out the pain. As he lay moaning, the answer suddenly came to him. "If I tell you," he wheezed, "you have to promise me something."

Clyde raised his eyebrows. Jack had never tried this tactic with him—not once. But maybe it wasn't just a tactic...maybe it was the truth. "I don't have to promise you anything," Clyde snarled.

"Suit yourself."

Clyde roared and gave the poor youth another round of blows. "Tell me!" he demanded. "Tell me where it is!"

Jack didn't give him the satisfaction of an answer, which enraged Clyde even more. Finally, with his fists bloodied and Jack left almost for dead on the cold floor, Clyde collected himself. "Well," he said, struggling to contain his anger, "what do I have to do to get this map? Huh?"

"You can't touch Hayley." Jack spoke between bloody teeth, every syllable painful to speak. "If you so much as lay a finger on her, your precious map is lost to me."

"So you do have it."

"In my mind, yes."

Clyde smiled evilly. "So be it," he said.

Jack rolled onto his side and spit a mixture of blood and saliva onto the floor. "One more thing," he rasped. "My memory of the map comes in bits and pieces, so I need something to trigger it. I need to set foot on an island."

Clyde narrowed his eyes. "Even if we do venture onto an island, there's no chance of you escaping."

"I'm not using this to escape." Jack was bluffing, but not to possibly get away from Clyde. He just wanted to talk to Hayley. If Clyde could agree to sparing Hayley and to visiting a deserted island, Jack would be able to convince him to allow a bit of privacy.

"It's a deal," Clyde said suddenly.

It was obvious how much Clyde's enthrallment with the treasure was getting to him, so Jack fished for more. "And to make sure you don't hurt Hayley, you need to bring her with me on the island."

Clyde pursed his lips, contemplating the new twist in the deal. A leery smile stretched across his face. "My word's not good enough for you?"

"I'll never trust you."

The words were spoken with such venom that Clyde took a step back. His dark eyes met Jack's blue orbs. Neither looked away. "Fine," Clyde spat. "We'll do it your way. But one trick on your part, and the girl's dead."

"So be it." Jack peered up at Clyde through a newly-forming black eye. "What are we waiting for?"

Chapter 18

Even though Jack's note had specifically told Hayley not to worry, she found it impossible to do otherwise. Clyde and his men had guns. Jack was unarmed. Who knew what they were doing to him in Clyde's quarters?

She shuddered just thinking about it. The next day, as she headed upstairs to the dining hall for lunch, she was so immersed in her thoughts that she didn't hear the footsteps behind her. Suddenly, a large, meaty hand clamped over her mouth. Her eyes grew wide with fear when the cold barrel of a gun pressed into the small of her back.

"Keep walking," the man said, just low enough for Hayley to pick out his Spanish accent. "We're going up on deck."

Hayley's hands shook as she followed the man's orders. Though his gun was put away and he was following at a farther distance, she was too afraid to make a run for it. She made her way across the deck to the railing, where she stood waiting for directions.

The Spaniard came up beside her. "See that island?"

Hayley nodded numbly. Already some of the passengers were piling into rowboats, ready to be ferried onshore. Many were eager to visit the final island before returning to the harbor tomorrow morning. Those who had yet to eat lunch were milling about the deck, but nobody was suspicious of Hayley and the surly-looking man next to her.

"That's where you're goin'," he said in a low voice.

Hayley's face twitched in surprise. What?

"Once you see Clyde, meet him in one of the boats and stay there. He'll tell you what to do next."

I'm going to the island? What happened to staying on The Queen Francis? What happened to all those death threats?

"Did you hear me?"

"Yes," Hayley squeaked.

The Spaniard backed off, just far enough away to still assert his presence and remind Hayley not to goof off. She watched the other passengers until her eyes alighted on Clyde. Jack and two other men were with them. Hayley sucked in a deep breath and made her way across the deck.

"Nice of you to join us, Cat Eyes," Clyde said with a sour laugh. Hayley didn't reply. When she glanced over at Jack, his features nearly took her breath away. He was obviously wearing makeup to cover a beastly black eye and several bruises. Hayley's stomach clenched.

"It's not as bad as it looks," he whispered. Before Hayley could reply, they were hustled into a rowboat and separated by one of Clyde's men. They were off to the island.

Once on shore, Clyde set off for a secluded part of the beach. He made sure no tourists or crew were watching before disappearing around a bank, out of sight. Jack and Hayley, forced to follow him, jogged across the sand with the Spaniard and Sully right behind them.

Unlike Jack's island, this isle was significantly smaller and had less foliage. It was just a rolling mound of sand dotted with a few palm trees and bushes. Large boulders made for convenient hiding places, however, and Clyde made sure his group went undetected.

Finally, underneath the shade of a palm, he bent down and looked Jack squarely in the eye. "I kept my part of the deal," he growled. "Now it's your turn."

"Patience," Jack said coolly, which caused Clyde to curse in frustration.

"You got five minutes, Nau."

"I get all the time I need."

Clyde cursed again. Hayley watched as Jack closed his eyes, his face a look of pure concentration. After a few minutes, he reopened his eyes and shrugged. "I got nothing."

"You lied!" Clyde roared.

"I need more time," Jack insisted. "Trust me, I can't just will the map to appear on my own. It only comes in certain moments."

The Spaniard walked over and murmured something in Clyde's ear. "Fine," he said sourly. "What kind of 'certain moments' do you need?"

Jack cocked his head to one side. "Well...if you and your men leave for a few minutes, I might be able to get the concentration I need."

Yeah, right, Hayley thought. To her surprise, Clyde conceded. "Tie them together," he ordered. Sully quickly produced a rope from his pocket and told Jack and Hayley to sit back-to-back. He tied both of their hands together, then their ankles (separately), before reminding them to stay out of sight. "If you don't," he warned for the umpteenth time, "we shoot the girl."

"Fair enough," Jack said, a little too lightheartedly for Hayley's liking. Once Clyde and his lackeys had disappeared around the bank, he began rubbing his wrists together.

"Trying to escape, Houdini?" Hayley asked.

"No, just loosening the rope enough to turn around. I have an idea."

She pursed her lips together. "Well, let's hurry. I don't know how long we have before they come back."

They struggled with the rope for a few more minutes until Jack had some slack. He and Hayley could now sit side-by-side instead of back-to-back. They awkwardly scooted into position. "Can you raise your outer hand?" Jack asked.

"I think so."

"On the count of three." Together, they raised their hands and brought them over their heads. Now they could easily sit next to each other without putting strain on their arms. "There," Jack said. "That wasn't so hard."

"I still think we should hurry. What's your idea?"

"Okay, so you obviously know Clyde is after a treasure map. He believes I have it."

"One sec. Now that our hands are almost free, shouldn't we try to untie our ankles and just make a run for it?"

"Listen," Jack insisted, speaking faster with excitement. "Where would we run to? We'd never make it around the corner without them shooting you."

Hayley sighed, knowing he was right. "Anyway," he continued, "Clyde believes I have the map he's looking for. I didn't, and I kept telling him that. Not until I was left on that deserted island did I realize I did have the map after all. I've had it this whole time."

"What?"

"It's confusing. I think the map is in my head. It's not physical. It's like a memory or something."

Hayley couldn't help but laugh. "How could you not remember your own memories?"

"It didn't make sense to me, either. Plus, I only get glimpses of it during certain times, like if I shut and open my eyes or look at something close-up and then something far away. It's weird."

Hayley stared long and hard at him. She was still having a hard time imagining him as the rough-and-tough caveman from a few days ago. The words slipped out of her mouh almost subconsciously. "You mean, like a camera lens?"

"What?"

"You said yourself you can only see the map during certain times. The way you described it made me imagine your eyes focusing in and out like a camera lens."

Jack let that soak in for a moment. "My God, Hayley, I think you're onto something."

"Try it," she urged. "Grab that twig over there."

Jack struggled to reach the twig, which was just slightly within his reach. Once he had it gripped between two fingers, he held it in front of his face.

"Stare at it for a few seconds, then switch your eyes to the palm tree over there. Your vision should automatically focus in and out depending on what you're looking at."

Jack was fascinated. He stared at the twig, then at the palm tree directly behind it thirty yards away. "It's working!" he gasped. His eyes seemed to be focusing on something else now. His pupils darted from side to side. He repeated the steps for a few moments, his smile growing larger each second. Hayley couldn't help but smile as well. Jack looked like a little kid in a candy store.

"I still don't get how you can see it," she said. "Is it in your mind or something? If your eyes are focusing in and out, the image should be phys—"

Jack suddenly turned to face Hayley, his eyes glowing with excitement. "You're a lifesaver!" he exclaimed, grabbing her hand triumphantly.

Hayley didn't know how discovering a treasure map was lifesaving—after all, this was the same map Clyde was after, and he seemed intent on killing them once they gave him what he wanted. She tried to scoot away, her cheeks flaming at such close contact with Jack, but the rope prevented her from doing so.

Jack suddenly realized how close he was, too, but he didn't try to pull away. His gaze flickered across her features, taking in her vibrant green eyes and sharp, defined cheekbones. He closed his eyes and smiled.

Hayley couldn't deny that holding hands with Jack was comforting. She felt his reassurance wash over her, and she closed her eyes dreamily. In a nanosecond, a bright light swept over her vision. A jumble of letters and images flickered past. Hayley quickly jerked her hand out of Jack's.

"Whoa!" he exclaimed. "Did you see that? Tell me you saw that."

"I saw it," she said. "I just don't believe it."

Jack's jaw dropped open. "Wait, are you serious?"

"I don't know. I think I saw something like a map—those symbols and letters...a blinding light..."

He sucked in a deep breath. "This is insane."

In reply, Hayley grabbed his hand and closed her eyes. Once again, she savored the moment, trying not to concentrate on the physical contact but on the words and images flashing through her mind. Of all the symbols she saw, only one was sharp enough to actually see and remember. Hayley opened her eyes and let go of his hand.

"Wow," Jack said, breathless. "Did you see it again?"

"You bet I did." Hayley's eyes glowed with excitement. She awkwardly twisted her body to grab the twig out of his hands. She proceeded to draw in the hard-packed sand. Because her hands were still tied, though loosely, she couldn't draw as well as she'd like to. But her picture was clear to Jack.

"Is that what you saw?" he asked.

"Yes. I don't know what to make of it." Her crude picture looked like some sort of trapezoid with an open top.

"Give me the stick," Jack ordered, suddenly lacking any of his light humor from earlier. Hayley obediently passed the twig, and he improved on her picture by draw a half-circle on top of the trapezoid. "There. What does that look like to you?"

"A seashell," she said, surprised. "Like the ones from scallops. But how...?"

"I saw it too. The first symbol—the clearest symbol—was this half-circle."

"And the first symbol I saw was this trapezoid thing."

They stared at each other. "Wow," Hayley breathed. "I can't believe it...it's like we have two different parts of the map, and they both fit together."

"Does this give me an excuse to hold hands with you again?"

"Not unless I give you permission."

Jack grinned. "Fair enough."

"What do you think the seashell means?"

"I don't know. It could mean anything."

"Maybe—"

Suddenly, Clyde and his lackeys burst around the corner. "Time's up," he growled. "I hope you have something to show me, Nau, or the girl's gone."

"That wasn't the deal," Jack said, quickly reaching out with his foot and swiping the drawing of the shell clear. "Besides, I think you'll be happy to know that—"

Upon seeing their loosened bonds, Clyde marched over and silenced Jack with a slap. He grabbed the collar of Hayley's shirt and yanked her to her feet, which forced Jack to his feet as well. "I said no funny business," Clyde roared, "or the girl gets killed!"

Jack didn't even flinch. "As I was saying—"

"My gun, Billings," Clyde demanded. One of his men strode forward and placed the Glock in Clyde's open palm.

Jack's eyes widened just a fraction. "Wefoundthemap!"

This was obviously good news. Clyde let go of Hayley's collar and stepped back. "Untie them," he ordered. Once the men had freed Jack and Hayley from the ropes, Clyde handed the Glock back to Billings.

"So you found the map."

His hostages nodded vigorously.

"Where do we go?" Clyde asked.

Hayley, still in shock, was glad that Jack answered for both of them in his steady voice. "An island," he said simply. "An island in the shape of a scallop shell."

Chapter 19

Clyde waited until all the passengers and crew from The Queen Francis left the island before radioing a friend. A few hours later, his private boat, the Antonia, came into view. Jack and Hayley were hustled onboard, followed by Clyde and the rest of the men. Since Clyde didn't have to worry about dealing with civilians anymore, he had free reign to do what he wanted. His first step was to search for a shell-shaped island somewhere in the Caribbean—which was no easy feat.

Everyone, it seemed, was affected by this turn of events. Clyde and his men had renewed energy and vigor. Though they still treated their captives with contempt, they also realized Hayley and Jack were their only link to finding treasure. Without them, the map was lost.

Hayley still missed her Gran and wished things could back to the way they were. On the upside, she was no longer showered with death threats. She and Jack were allowed a few moments together after Jack explained he had linked Hayley to part of the map. Though this had enraged Clyde, he quickly realized he had no other choice but to keep Hayley alive—and thus, keep his dreams of becoming a millionaire alive too.

Jack was his usual self—cocky, unafraid, and always guarded. If anything, he seemed just as excited as Clyde to find the treasure. Linking with Hayley added an extra punch to his attitude (or maybe that was from holding hands with her. Hayley could never figure him out).

Jack and Hayley both knew they were at risk, however. Jack had taken a shot in the dark by assuming the shell-shaped island was their destination for the treasure. With no coordinates or directions to go by, Clyde and his men pored over various maps searching for an island that fit Jack's description.

Hayley and Jack spoke as often as they could. Their conversations usually centered around the mysterious map and why Clyde had suddenly switched from The Queen Francis to the Antonia. They always had at least one of his lackeys watching them, however, so they had to guard their words.

"I still think it's weird," Hayley said, just low enough for Jack to hear. "Why didn't Clyde send for his boat days ago? Why even risk exposing us on The Queen Francis?"

Jack had to admit he was stumped too. "Maybe he couldn't radio his ship in time. I don't know. I'm pretty sure the Antonia is the same one he used to leave me on that island for six months."

"Then it doesn't make sense to use The Queen Francis. Why would Clyde want to mess with civilians on a tour boat? Why would he risk having one of his men bribe the captain to visit your island?"

Jack snapped his fingers. "That's it! Why would Clyde want to mess with civilians on a tour boat?"

"I just said that."

"Think, Hayley. He surrounded himself—hid himself—in a tour boat while searching for treasure. Why?" He lowered his voice. "Because he's not the only one who's searching."

Hayley nodded thoughtfully. It made sense that there were other men out there, men like Clyde, who were looking for this treasure and would stop at nothing to get it. "Are you sure you're the only one with the map?"

"I'm positive. This isn't the first time I've been kidnapped by treasure hunters. I've been on the run for years."

"So Clyde must have wanted to keep a low profile and not attract attention. The Queen Francis was the perfect disguise."

Suddenly, the door burst open, and Clyde strode in from the deck.

"Speak of the devil," Jack muttered. Fortunately, Clyde didn't hear him. The man who had been in charge of watching Jack and Hayley quickly jumped to attention.

"Good news, boys," Clyde said, eyes shining. "We found ourselves the only shell-shaped island in the Caribbean. We got ourselves a half-days' journey, and then it's treasure time."

Chapter 20

Oliver peered over the railing at the swirling turquoise waters. Small whitecaps lapped at the hull of the boat, creating miniature whirlpools and eddies. The Queen Francis cruised through the crystal-clear ocean, heading back to the harbor where it had first set sail.

Oliver couldn't deny that he was happy. He felt like a fool for following Hayley and nearly having a nervous breakdown on the island. This is the first and last boat trip I'll ever take, he told himself. There was something about the refreshing sea breeze and placid waters that appealed to him, though. He found that he couldn't tear his gaze away from the drifting ocean. He had often spent nights staring into the sunset, watching as bold streaks of color were painted across the surface of the water. It inspired him and filled him with a peace he didn't know existed. It almost wiped out any thoughts of Hayley.

He frowned and pushed away from the railing. He had worked his tail off trying not to be seen by her. A sour mixture of shame and regret churned in his stomach. He wished he had never set foot on The Queen Francis. Following Hayley was a mistake, and he knew it. He had often thought of what would happen if she found out he had shadowed her. In each scenario played out in his head, the result was the same: anger.

"I'm such an idiot," he muttered. Two women suddenly brushed past his shoulders, talking excitedly in hushed whispers. Oliver's cheeks flushed as he realized he might have spoken a bit too loud.

Bits and pieces of the women's conversation reached his ears: "...gone missing..." "...luggage still in her room..." "...Captain's trying to keep it quiet..."

Oliver shivered. Someone was missing? That's ridiculous, he thought. But when he entered the dining hall the next morning, he was surprised to see everyone on the edge of their seats rather than chatting lightly about the trip. It was the final day aboard The Queen Francis, and yet all the passengers seemed jittery.

Oliver floated past the tables to the buffet line. His arms were peppered with goosebumps when he heard, "She disappeared last night. She left everything behind—all her luggage, her books, everything."

"But not a suicide note," someone else spoke up. "You'd think if she had jumped overboard, she would leave a note saying why."

"What if she didn't jump overboard?" another passenger argued. "She's not the only one missing, you know. A group of men vanished along with her."

"I don't believe it," the first person said stiffly. "The crew's just telling stories to scare us."

"I'm just glad we're going home today. I've had too much adventure for one week."

Oliver was officially spooked. He looked left and right, sweeping his gaze over the dining hall like he had done many times before. This time, however, he wasn't looking to avoid Hayley—he needed to find her.

She was nowhere in sight.

Chapter 21

From sea level, the island looked nothing like a scallop shell. All Jack could see were monstrous cliffs and thousands of razor-sharp rocks. It seemed like the entire island was fringed by these protruding canines, which reminded Jack of a shark's mouth wide open and ready to bite.

Clyde directed the boat to the opposite side of the island. It seemed to be at least four miles long. Finally, they spotted an opening between the treacherous rocks. "We'll anchor in the bay," Clyde said.

Jack got a glimpse of Clyde's map just before he was hustled over to Hayley, his arms pinned behind his back. From the map's perspective, the island was obviously shaped like a scallop shell, but its other features were uncharted.

"What do we do now?" Hayley asked in a low whisper.

"We wait," Jack said. He squinted through the bright sunlight at the looming island in front of them. All he could see were rocks, glittering white sand, dense jungle, and towering cliffs.

Well, he thought, if there was one perfect place to bury pirates' treasure, this would be it. The entire island screamed 'mysterious.' There was an air of anticipation about it. The landmass seemed to be shrouded in deceptive beauty.

A few men were left onboard with instructions to radio Clyde in 5 days. The rest went with Clyde, Jack, and Hayley to the island. It was a smooth ride to the bay, and once onshore, Jack thought he had never felt sand so soft. He gazed left and right, wondering how a place could look so raw and untouched. At the same time, the island seemed to be alive with energy. Jack knew this was it. Every cell in his body told him the treasure was here.

Clyde could sense it as well. His eyes flickered everywhere, probing the lush foliage and sandstone cliffs as if, somehow, the treasure was in plain sight. "All right," he said, "we made it. Where to now?"

Jack and Hayley glanced at each other. She looked afraid and confused. Jack wished he could comfort those pleading green eyes. "Ready?" he whispered.

She nodded. "Untie us," Jack demanded.

Clyde rolled his eyes, but motioned for his men to undo the ropes. As soon as their hands were free, Jack took Hayley's hand in his, and they closed their eyes.

The effect was instantaneous. Rather than seeing a jumble of words and symbols, the shape of a triangle emerged in their minds. Hayley gasped and let go of Jack's hand. "It's in French!" she exclaimed.

"I'm not sure if I saw all of the word," Jack said, opening his eyes. "I saw a triangle, and then R-I-V-I-something. It could be French."

"That's all?" Clyde frowned. "Did you see any landmarks?"

They shook their heads, causing Clyde to curse. "Whatever you just did, do it again," he demanded.

They obeyed. This time, Jack was able to see the entire word: rivière. Hayley said her word was argentée. Everyone automatically looked around the group, wondering who was able to translate.

"Fantastic," Clyde said. "Nobody knows French, and yet our only clues leading to the map happen to be in French."

Jack knew things were going to get ugly unless they made some more progress. Despite his mild fear, he was excited. He had never spoken French in his life, and yet here was some strange French word, embedded in his mind.

"Anyone?" Clyde asked, his voice rising. "Does anyone know French?"

"I think the first word means 'river,'" Sully spoke up.

Clyde snorted. "Thank you for your valuable insight." He turned to Jack. "Did you see anything else?"

"No," Jack said. "We can only view one part of the map at a time."

"How convenient."

"That's the way it is."

Clyde looked like he was going to explode from frustration. "If someone here speaks French, tell me NOW."

Suddenly, Hayley cleared her throat. "I do."

Everyone, including Jack, looked at her in surprise. Shy, scared Hayley Slade was speaking up? They couldn't believe it.

"Finally!" Clyde roared. "What does it mean?"

"I only took a few semesters in school, but I know enough to hold a conversation," she said quietly. "Rivière argentée translates to 'silver river.'"

"Thank you," Clyde spat. He glared at his men. "Well, what are you waiting for? Spread out and look for a silver river!"

Hayley and Jack were whisked away by the Spaniard, who stomped across the sand towards the jungle. The other men scattered in all directions. Within minutes came hoots and hollers from the other side of the bay. Someone had found a river.

"Hey! Over here!" a man yelled. Everyone eagerly rushed over. "There's no actual silver," he explained, "but the bottom is definitely a silver color."

Clyde looked disappointed, Jack could tell. He had probably been looking forward to the prospect of mining silver. "All right," Clyde said. "Now what?"

Jack reached over and grabbed Hayley's hand. Her cheeks were flushed and her hair was matted across her sweaty forehead. She gave him a halfhearted smile just before they closed their eyes. Upon reopening them a few moments later, both Jack and Hayley wore mirrored looks of confusion.

"What's the problem?" Clyde barked.

"There's nothing new," Jack said. "Together, we both see rivière argentée. The other clues haven't been revealed."

The men grumbled. Clyde stepped up to Jack and spat at his feet. "You're trying my patience, Nau," he growled.

"Cool your jets. We've only been on this island for ten minutes. Maybe we're not supposed to just stand here and stare at the river. Maybe we should follow it."

Jack's logic made sense to the other men, and before long they created two winding lines on both sides of the river. They hiked for half an hour, studying the cool, babbling waters for any clues or bits of treasure floating downstream. The Silver River, as they called it, meandered through the jungle to the base of the cliffs, where it ended in a roaring waterfall.

Slick with sweat, Jack lay down on the bank and dipped his head in the stream, far enough from the waterfall to avoid any of the churning eddies. Where the river met the waterfall, a large pool had formed, fringed by boulders and dark moss. Jack glanced up to the top of the cliffs. They seemed to stretch higher than a skyscraper, and with no jagged footfalls or ledges, they were inaccessible.

"I guess our journey ends here," Hayley said quietly, scooting close to Jack. She, too, peered up at the towering cliffs. "If we weren't in such a dire situation, I would love to take a swim under the waterfall."

Jack smiled. At least she was getting a sense of humor back. He loved seeing her unafraid. "Don't worry. Clyde can't hurt us. We're his only link to the treasure, remember?"

"I guess. But it's not working."

Jack had to admit he was stumped, too. Why would the clue lead them to the Silver River when they didn't know what to do from there?

Sully and a few other men took off their shirts and waded into the stream. Clyde paced back and forth along the riverbank, his forehead creased in anger. Jack pushed himself off the ground, shook out his wet hair, and walked a few paces downstream. He knew he was missing something. If the clue said Silver River, then the Silver River it was.

Jack stayed in sight of Clyde and his men as he continued to walk. He peered at the crystal-clear water, which bubbled over small rocks and lapped at the banks. The bottom certainly did give the water a silver glow. Was it granite? Quartz? Jack had never been good at identifying rocks and minerals.

Suddenly, as his gaze flickered across the river bottom, he caught sight of a small carving in the rock. He rolled up his jeans and carefully waded into the middle of the river. Though the water rose far past his waist, the current wasn't too strong, so he had no problem staying in one spot. He peered down at the triangle carved into the rock at the bottom. "What in the world...?" he muttered. He took a deep breath and ducked underwater. Particles of sand, dirt, and tiny bits of grass floated past him. He placed his hands on the bottom to steady himself as he observed the strange carving. He thought he could make out the word roche. French, again?

Jack pushed off the bottom and resurfaced. He pulled himself back onto the riverbank and shook out his wet hair. "Hayley!"

His voice attracted her and Clyde's attention. She rushed over, confused and anxious. "What is it?"

Without replying, Jack grabbed her hand and closed his eyes. Immediately, the insides of his eyelids flooded with light, and another word flashed across his vision: pois.

"Did you see that?" he asked once they had let go.

Hayley nodded excitedly. "The letter à," she said.

"I saw pois. What does thatmean?" Jack asked, spelling it out in case he had mispronounced it.

"Pois? Um...polka dots? I think."

"How about roche?"

"Now that I know. It means 'rock.'"

Jack felt stupid. Of course he would find the word "rock" carved onto a rock at the bottom of the river. Maybe he was on the wrong path. Then again, after finding roche, he and Hayley had been given access to the next clue. They had to be on the right track after all.

She snapped her fingers just as Clyde walked over. "Wait, I got it!"

"The next clue?" he asked hopefully.

"Jack, pois doesn't necessarily mean 'polka dots.' With my letter à, all three words join together to form roche à pois, which means 'spotted rock.'"

Clyde grinned. "Finally! Is that all?"

Jack and Hayley exchanged a glance. "I guess so," Jack said. "Our next clue is a spotted rock, so judging by the millions of rocks on this Godforsaken island, it shouldn't be hard to find at all."

His sarcasm didn't go unnoticed.

Chapter 22

T he sky was tinted orange by the time Hayley and her group of men—led by the Spaniard—returned to the Silver River. Though everyone was weary from the day's events, morale was still high. The treasure was somewhere on the island. It was only a matter of time.

Hours earlier, Clyde had organized his men into three groups. Some searched the bay area, some hiked along the base of the cliffs, and others trekked through the jungle. They had searched almost the entire island for the roche à pois, the 'spotted rock,' with no such luck. Everyone had returned to the Silver River just before nightfall.

To Hayley's dismay, she didn't get a chance to speak to Jack for the rest of the evening. They had been separated during the search, and it seemed Clyde had made it his personal duty to separate them again—for punishment, maybe? Clyde had been uncharacteristically calm and collected all afternoon.

"Tomorrow," he said as the men built a campfire, "we find the roche à pois."

Hayley was rudely awakened the next morning. The Spaniard shook her shoulders more forcefully than an earthquake. She sat up and grumbled to herself, already feeling hunger pains. Though everyone had eaten last night, the meal had hardly been satisfactory. Clyde had put his men on strict rations. Their water supply was taken care of thanks to the Silver River, but they only had as much food as was in their backpacks. So far, they hadn't seen a single sign of game. There were no fruit trees, either.

"It's as if this island was made to protect the treasure," Hayley remembered Jack saying. "Think about it: the island's surrounded by dangerous rocks, there's no food available, and the cliffs are keeping us from exploring the northeast coast."

If I was a pirate, Hayley thought, this would definitely be the place to bury my treasure.

After a quick and unsatisfactory breakfast, Clyde split the men into three groups again. He gave each group slightly different directions. Everyone was to meet back at the Silver River by noon.

Hayley was in the second group, which meant she was forced to go across the river. She had traveled that way last night but hadn't found anything resembling a spotted rock. Though no one in her group spoke to her, she could almost feel their frustration in the air. She suspected they thought she'd lied to them—after all, she was the only one who spoke French. She could easily lead them off track and make up clues.

Minutes turned into hours, and before long Hayley's throat felt like the Sahara. She needed water badly, but she was afraid to ask for fear of being ridiculed. The men pushed doggedly through the jungle. The thick humidity made their hair stick to their foreheads. Sweat poured down their necks. The buzz of mosquitoes and other insects filled the air.

Suddenly, they reached a clearing. The large palm trees that had blocked the sun were now gone. Hayley didn't feel closed in anymore, but the heat was still intense. She nearly cried out in relief when she spotted the ocean, dotted with the island's noticeable defense mechanism—the pointed rocks.

The group descended a large bank, their feet sinking into the warm sand. The golden mounds soon gave way to hard, brittle rock, which in turn gave way to solid rock that dipped towards the ocean. They were approaching a series of tide pools.

Hayley copied the men's movements and took off her shoes. She carefully waded into the cool water, making sure she wasn't stepping on any sea creatures in the process. Despite the glaring sun and pouring sweat, she felt refreshed. It was amazing what a little water could do.

The men's conversations automatically lightened. Instead of grumbling to one another, they relaxed and chatted about what they would do once they found the treasure. Hayley thought it ridiculous that they were already planning so far ahead. She had never actually brought herself to imagine what would happen once they found the treasure. What would Clyde think of Hayley and Jack then? Would he kill them?

Hayley shuddered. She bent over and poked a sea anemone, which retracted upon contact. With a jolt, she realized she missed Jack. She wanted to hear his confident voice and see his strong features. He was her source of comfort in this crazy nightmare.

"Hey! Over here!"

Everyone's heads snapped up, including Hayley's. The men stopped what they were doing to watch the Spaniard, who pointed excitedly towards the jungle. "Look!"

There, jutting out from the palm trees, was a huge spotted boulder. It was wedged between the cliffs and the tide pools, about eight or nine feet in width and thrice as tall. Compared to all the other rocks Hayley had seen, this one clearly fit the description of the roche à pois.

Within seconds, the men dashed from the tide pools and stampeded towards the spotted rock. Some whooped and smacked the Spaniard on the back, exulting over his discovery. Hayley watched from a distance, still wading in the tide pool. She lifted a hand to shade her eyes from the sun. There was no doubt about it—they had found the Spotted Rock.

A few of the men tried to climb up and over the boulder to see if there were any markings. Disappointed, they soon gave up and prepared to head back to the Silver River.

"Oi, girl!" one of them shouted. "Time to go!"

Hayley obediently slipped on her shoes and walked over. As usual, she avoided eye contact with Clyde's goonies. It didn't stop one of the men from addressing her, unfortunately.

"What's our next clue?" he demanded.

"I don't know," she said timidly.

"What do you mean, you don't know? I thought you were supposed to see the map!"

Hayley backed away timidly.

"Billings, leave her alone," the Spaniard ordered. "Once we get that treasure, we can have fun with her. First we need to regroup and find Jack. Then we can get the next clue."

Billings muttered something under his breath and stormed away. Hayley didn't realize she had been holding her breath until she felt lightheaded. She turned and leaned against the Spotted Rock. I want to go home. As she studied the brown and gray spots, she thought she saw something embedded in the boulder's grainy surface. Was that a triangle?

The closer she looked, the more she came to realize it wasn't just a trick of the light. She actually did see a triangle. Letters slowly materialized in the center, forming the word chute. Hayley gasped in surprise.

"What?" the Spaniard snapped. "What is it?"

Hayley shook her head. "I don't know!"

"Tell me."

"A clue," she squeaked. "I think it says chute."

The men immediately gathered around. Hayley closed her eyes and wished she didn't sound so afraid. She needed to be strong, especially when she was apart from Jack. "I found part of the next clue," she said, louder this time. Her voice held no waver. "The word is chute, which means to slide or fall."

The Spaniard smiled darkly. "Excellent," he said. "Let's head back to the River, boys!"

The return trip seemed to take less time than it did to reach the tide pools. Hayley was weak from hunger and thirst, and she felt like her entire body had emptied its sweat glands. She perspired from head to toe. The men walked at such a fast pace that she fell behind multiple times. Finally, they reached the Silver River, where they met up with the first group. They looked exhausted and defeated, but once the Spaniard explained they had found the Spotted Rock, morale skyrocketed.

Hayley was ushered forward. "Where's Jack?" the Spaniard demanded. In a matter of seconds, Jack was shoved forward from his group, and he gave Hayley a reassuring smile.

"Good job," he said. "I'm assuming you're the one who found the clue?"

"They're the ones who found the rock," she replied. "I just saw the clue."

"Then let's find the other half."

They joined hands. Hayley was now used to the thrill that ran up her arm whenever their fingers touched. Together, they closed their eyes. Hayley's eyelids immediately flooded with light. Letters and symbols flickered across her vision until they slowed down to form two characters: d'.

Jack spelled out his word: E-A-U. Hayley quickly pieced the two together to form the French translation of 'water': d'eau.

"Well, this is unexpected," she said.

"Why?"

"We got lucky with this clue. Any guesses on what chute d'eau means?"

Jack grinned. "Waterslide."

"Close. Try waterfall."

The men whooped and hollered. All of them dashed over to the Silver River, flinging off their shoes and diving into the pool that formed the base of the waterfall. Jack and Hayley watched as they swam underneath the roaring turbulence, only to resurface empty-handed.

"They never learn," Jack said. "When are they going to realize only one of us can see the next clue?"

Hayley laughed. "I'm parched. Want to get something to drink?"

They walked over to the pool and lay down. Kneeling on the riverbank, they cupped their hands and drank for a good minute before getting to their feet.

"Me or you?" Jack asked.

"You. I'm not that good at swimming," Hayley said.

Jack nodded and kicked off his shoes. He pulled his shirt over his head and rolled up his jeans. Hayley watched his corded muscles ripple as he dove in. The men automatically made way for Jack, who swam directly under the waterfall and disappeared from sight. After a few moments, he resurfaced, flipping his wet hair over his forehead. "I got it!" he announced.

Hayley jogged over to the edge closest to the waterfall. She tried not to look as Jack pulled himself over the bank, biceps bulging. Her cheeks flushed.

"You're not gonna believe this," he said. "It's d'eau again. On the other side of the waterfall was a smooth cliff face. I saw a triangle and the word d'eau."

"That's strange," Hayley said.

Jack shrugged, his shoulders glistening with water droplets. He stuck out his hand. "Ready to give it a go?"

Hayley gripped his fingers tightly, ignoring the pulsing excitement that rushed through her body at their contact. She tried to focus on the letters arranging themselves in her head: tte. Obviously, that had to be the suffix of a word.

"G-R-O," Jack said once they reopened their eyes.

"Grotte," Hayley responded. "Like a grotto or cave."

"Water cave?" Jack asked.

"Water cave," she confirmed.

"Great. Another broad clue. We're entirely surrounded by water, and yet the map wants us to find a water cave."

"Maybe we don't have to look very far," Hayley said quietly. She didn't know why Jack was so eager to find the treasure. Didn't that imply a death sentence for the two of them?

"What do you mean?"

"How well did you check the area surrounding the waterfall? I mean, look up there." She pointed to the top of the cliffs. A large pile of rocks was placed on either side of the start of the waterfall. "Doesn't it look like someone made a dam?"

Jack's eyes widened. "Yeah. Maybe someone directed the stream to this part of the cliffs—"

"—because they wanted to cover the grotto," Hayley finished. They grinned.

Jack placed one foot on the edge of the bank. "How do you feel about going for a swim now?"

Chapter 23

The refreshing water cleansed Jack's pores as if someone had taken a hose and squirted all his sweat away. He closed his eyes and slowly floated to the surface. He felt cleansed and ready to tackle the next obstacle—finding the grotte d'eau, or water cave.

Just as he resurfaced, someone gave a short cry and cannonballed into the water next to him. He flipped the hair out of his eyes and smiled. "Glad you could join me."

Hayley came up sputtering. "I didn't expect it to be this c-cold," she said. Plastered against her skin, her hair and clothes gave her the appearance of a drowning rat. To Jack, though, she had never looked prettier. He quickly looked away.

"I'm not that confident of a swimmer," Hayley added. "Can you dive down first and tell me how long I have to hold my breath?"

"Yeah, of course." Jack took a few strokes toward the waterfall and ducked underneath the surface. He could barely see through the churning foam, but once he had safely swam to the other side, the water was a crystal, cerulean color. He scissor-kicked his way over to the rock wall where he had seen the word d'eau just minutes earlier. Now it was gone.

The waterfall continued to crash behind him, sending shockwaves of water toward this area of the pool. Placing his hands on the wall, Jack kept himself from floating upwards as he took in his surroundings. No matter how hard he looked, though, he didn't see anything resembling an underwater cave or grotto. There was nothing but the rocky walls, mossy bottom, and green banks.

Jack could feel his lungs craving oxygen. He knew he had about half a minute left. He pushed off the wall and swam to the bottom. Wedged between the cliff and mossy floor was a pile of rocks. Jack thought it odd that rocks would collect here, of all places. Unless...

He quickly dove down and began pulling the rocks away. Thanks to the fluctuating water, he had no trouble loosening the pile and uncovering the human-sized tunnel that led through the cliff wall.

Jack grinned. Here we go, he thought. He pushed off the bottom, swam back underneath the waterfall, and resurfaced with his lungs near bursting.

"What did you see?" Sully demanded, not even waiting for Jack to catch his breath. The rest of the men crowded around, some in the water and some crouching on the river-bank.

"A tunnel," Jack wheezed. "At the bottom."

"What's in there?" Hayley asked tentatively.

"I don't know; I ran out of breath."

"Lead the way," Sully said. "I'm going down there with you."

Jack shook his head. "Not a good idea. The tunnel's only four feet wide and I didn't see where it goes. You're bigger than me. What if you get stuck?"

Sully realized Jack's logic. "All right," he conceded. "Hurry up."

Hayley nodded, her eyes pleading for Jack to be safe. After sucking in a huge gulp of air, Jack dove back down to the bottom. After forcing his way underneath the tumultuous waterfall, he made a beeline for the tunnel. He barely squeezed through the opening with his broad shoulders. A fleeting thought came to mind: What if there's no way out? It would be nearly impossible to force himself backwards through the narrow tunnel.

Jack squinted in the bleary underwater light. As he advanced, it only grew darker, and before long he couldn't even see the gray stone that served as walls all around him. His lungs started to burn, forcing him to swim faster. Just as he considered going backwards, fearing he was going to run out of air otherwise, the tunnel widened. Beams of light bounced off the rock walls, illuminating the way—straight up.

Jack had never tasted relief so sweet. He pushed off the bottom and ruptured the surface, gulping precious air. He dog-paddled over to the side and dragged himself onto a thin ledge. He'd made it.

After catching his breath, Jack took in his surroundings. Grotte d'eau was right—this certainly was a water cave. The rugged, black rock walls folded around him like a stone cathedral. The dark water glistened off the ceiling in luminous waves. A handful of tiny peepholes allowed slivers of sunlight to seep through. Jack was in awe. Was it possible he was the only human being to see this place in 300 years?

The thought crushed him like a thousand tons. He gripped the stone ledge, suddenly overcome with the seriousness of the situation. I've been treating this like a game. This whole time, I've been gambling with my life.

And Hayley's, the voice inside his head added. Jack grimaced.

He lifted his eyes to the ceiling, watching the water reflect off the rock, until a symbol materialized onto the stone surface. He got to his feet and studied it carefully.

Mort. A single word inside a triangle, just like the other clues. Jack let the word pass through his lips. "Mort...mortuary? Mortician? Mortifying?" To his educated mind, it reminded him of all things death-related. He shivered. How could such a dismal word be present in such a raw, untouched place?

Jack wrenched his eyes away and dove back into the water. He suddenly felt cold—freezing, almost. He swam as quickly as he could through the tunnel, under the waterfall, and towards the men. When he broke through the surface, shivering, he climbed onto the bank like a wet cat, ignoring the shouts of Clyde's men.

"Jack!" Hayley cried. She swam over to the side and pulled herself onto the grass. "What happened? You're so...pale."

He shook his head. "I don't know. I just needed to get out of there."

"You made it?"

"I made it," he confirmed. "The grotto was beautiful, but at the same time, it was…I don't know…dark."

Hayley placed a hand on his shoulder. Her stunning green eyes swam with worry. "Was there a clue?"

"Mort," he said quietly.

She pursed her lips. "Death."

"I thought as much."

Suddenly, Clyde stormed out of the jungle with his third group in tow. "You're back!" he said, his eyes alighting on Jack and Hayley.

"They found the next clue!" Sully exclaimed.

Clyde rushed over to the pair. "The spotted rock! Where was it?" he demanded.

Noticing the greedy glint in his eye and the way his hand hovered over his gun, Hayley spoke swiftly. "By the tide-pools," she said. "It led us back to the waterfall. Jack found a tunnel at the bottom of the pool that led to a grotte d'eau—a water grotto."

"And?" Clyde asked excitedly.

Jack and Hayley exchanged a glance. "Mort," she said finally. "Death."

Clyde appeared not to notice the gravity of her tone. "Perfect! What's the rest of the clue?"

Hayley glanced over at Jack, but he suddenly stood up and walked away, once again ignoring the shouts of Clyde's lackeys. He didn't bother to shake out his wet hair or put on his shoes as he strode into the jungle.

Chapter 24

Hayley felt deflated. She had just lost the one thing keeping her motivated and calm—Jack. She knew something had happened in the water grotto that spooked him. She could only hope he would return to his normal self.

Clyde stared at Jack's retreating figure as it disappeared into the shadows of the jungle. Cursing, he shouted, "Get him! He can't walk away now; not when we're so close!"

Hayley trembled when he placed a firm hand on her shoulder. "Did you find the rest of the clue, Cat Eyes?"

"N-No...Jack took off before we could hold hands."

"Isn't that cute," Clyde spat, his tone laden with sarcasm. It was revolting. "The clue just happens to 'reveal' itself when you're holding hands. I'm beginning to think you're just bluffing to keep me away from the treasure."

"I'm not!"

"And what about the fact that the clues happen to be in French? And you're the only one here who knows French?"

"I don't know, I swear—"

"I should kill you right now, you lying filth." Clyde grabbed Hayley's bicep and yanked her to her feet. She cried out, but was quickly silenced by the click of his Glock 19.

Suddenly, Sully's voice rang out in the air, clear as a bell. "We got 'im!" He and the Spaniard came stomping out of the jungle with Jack in between them. To Hayley's relief, Jack seemed unfazed by the whole situation until he saw the barrel of Clyde's gun pressed against her forehead.

"Hey!" He thrashed in the men's arms, forcing them to tighten their grip around his forearms. "You promised not to touch her!"

"You should know by now that I don't keep my promises," Clyde growled.

"Wait!" Jack cried, breathless. The Spaniard and Sully reluctantly let go, allowing Jack to sprint over to Hayley and stand between her and the gun. "You should know that if you pull that trigger, all your hopes of finding the treasure are gone."

"Get outta my way, Nau."

"Then kiss your rich dreams goodbye."

Clyde roared in anger and flung his gun on the ground, realizing Jack was right. He spat in the young man's face. "Just tell me the clue already! We have to be close!"

Hayley's eyes were wild with fear. She knew they were dealing with a madman now. The closer they got to the treasure, the sicker with greed Clyde would become.

When Jack tenderly held her hand, Hayley tried to focus on his piercing blue eyes. They were the color of the Caribbean, reminding her of pleasant evenings aboard The Queen Francis, staring into the sunset. Oh, Gran...

They closed their eyes. The next clue was brighter and bolder than all the rest. Clyde was right; they had to be close. It was only a matter of time...

The looming gray cliffs seemed to frown at Hayley. She felt so small compared to the immense structures. The Spaniard nudged her from behind, forcing her to keep moving.

"Don't be scared, Cat Eyes," he said.

How can I not be scared? she wanted to scream. As soon as she and Jack had discovered their next clue—arbre de la mort, Tree of Death—Clyde had wasted no time in searching for this Tree. Instead of splitting into groups, all the men had wandered the jungle for hours, finally returning to the Silver River for a rationed dinner. Now, it was twilight, and the first traces of moonlight spilled over the rocky paths near the cliffs. Clyde swore it was the quickest route to the other side of the island, where they would search the south jungle for some so-called Tree of Death.

In Hayley's opinion, she thought they should stay as far away from death as possible. She was even more afraid than usual now that Jack's charm had fizzled out. He looked weary and sullen through the glimpses of moonbeams that fell on his grizzled face.

Hayley wanted to cry. She would if she could, but her tears had long since dried out. She was hungry, thirsty, and fatigued. If only Clyde would tell them to stop and rest...

Suddenly, despite it already being dark, the entire world turned pitch black. For a second, Hayley thought her heavy eyelids had finally closed, and she had blacked out. But she could still hear shuffling feet and confused murmurs. Along with Jack, Clyde, and the other men, she looked up, expecting to see the shimmering half-moon that had been lighting their way.

She gasped. It had disappeared—or, more accurately, something was blocking it. Something big.

The group immediately scattered, stumbling in the darkness as they tried to stay on the path. Hayley was pushed to one side, where she finally caught sight of a sliver of the moon between large, gnarled branches. She cocked her head. Was that a tree?

"Hayley—is that you?" came a frantic whisper.

"Jack!"

"I can barely see you. Have you looked up?"

"Yes. I think there's a tree up there, at the top of the cliff."

"I know. I see it too."

They were drawn to each other's voice, and within seconds they had clasped hands. They both stared up at the huge, ominous object casting shadows on the path. "Do you think that's it?" Hayley asked.

"That's what?"

"The Tree."

"Oh. Maybe. I wish it was daylight so we could see it better. All I know is that it's awfully big."

Hayley drank in Jack's words as if they were life-giving oxygen. Why was it that his presence made her so calm? She drew closer to him so that their arms were touching. "Let's hope Clyde sets up camp for the night," she said.

As if reading her thoughts, Clyde did stay put and set up camp. The atmosphere was a mixture of excitement and uncertainty. Now that everyone knew what was blocking the moon, they all wondered if this was in fact the Tree of Death. It was easy to imagine the enormous, looming mass of branches as the fulfillment of that description, but what would it look like in broad daylight?

They found out the next morning. As the sun peeked over the edge of the cliffs, leaving their camp in shadow, Hayley roused. She saw Clyde and Sully arguing over something near the outskirts of the jungle. A few other men came walking down the path just before breakfast, lugging bottles of water they had filled from the Silver River.

Hayley and Jack had barely started on their meager meal together when Clyde hollered at Jack to come over. He obeyed, leaving Hayley to eat her fruit and hard-as-concrete bread in silence. She glanced over at the two men every so often. Within minutes, Clyde's face contorted to a deep purple color while Jack remained calm and indifferent.

Hayley wiped her mouth with the back of her hand and leaned back. Shading her eyes against the bright sun, she studied the Tree. It looked significantly less mysterious now, thoughts its size was still intimidating. Even from far away, its trunk was easily wider than the arm span of six men. Its gnarled branches stretched outwards in all directions, but life was obviously lacking. The entire tree was a dull brown color. There were no leaves or small plants growing at the base of the trunk, as far as Hayley could see. If there could be one symbol to represent the cold, unforgiving spirit of death, the Tree would be it.

She started at the sound of her name. Jack cupped his hands around his mouth and called her again. She stood up, dusted the dirt off her shorts, and hurried over. She didn't make eye contact with Clyde.

"We have a problem," he said stiffly. "If that's our next clue, we need to find some way to get up there."

Hayley let her eyes travel from the base of the cliff all the way to the top. She almost laughed out loud. There was no way.

"If one of you can get close enough, you might be able to see the clue," Clyde said. "There's a ledge not fifteen feet off the ground, and another one just above that. It zigzags almost all the way up the face of the cliff."

Hayley shaded her eyes and watched where Clyde pointed. There did seem to be thin ledges running horizontally across the stone. Still, it was crazy to think someone could actually climb up there.

"What if this isn't the Tree we're looking for?" Jack asked.

"You said it was!" Clyde exclaimed. "You have the map; you should know where the clues are!"

Hayley could tell this was a touchy subject.

"Get over there," Clyde demanded. When Jack didn't move, he hollered, "Go!" By now, he had attracted the attention of almost the entire camp.

Jack reluctantly made his way over to the base of the cliff. "I'm not climbing," he said.

"If you won't use those limbs of yours, I'll amputate them for you." Clyde grabbed a shotgun from one of his lackeys and pointed it at Jack. Hayley screamed, expecting to hear a gunshot at any moment.

Emotion suddenly sprung into Jack's lifeless eyes. Hayley knew he was afraid. "Wait! Don't," he said.

"Then start climbing!"

"I'm afraid of heights!"

"Start climbing!"

Hayley could tell by Jack's paralyzing fear that he was telling the truth. "Stop!" she cried. "He is afraid of heights! Didn't you hear him?"

"Too bad. He's got three seconds to use those limbs, or I make use of them myself." Clyde stepped forward, the shotgun still leveled.

Hayley was at the point of tears. "Please!"

Jack scrambled at the cliff, trying to make it onto the first ledge. After a few moments of grunting and struggling, he pulled himself up. His face was ashen. "I-I can't. I'm sorry," he stammered. He glanced up at the Tree, towering hundreds of yards above him, and nearly lost his balance. The action caused his face to turn even whiter.

Hayley gawked at him. Clyde was still aiming the shotgun at poor Jack, who had plastered himself against the stone like a ninja. He looked terrified.

"Keep moving!" Clyde roared.

"He can't!" Hayley cried. Sully and another man swiftly grabbed her, wrenching her away from the cliff. "Wait! Stop! Let me go instead!"

At last, Clyde lowered the gun and turned around. "What did you say?" he snapped.

Great, now I've really gone and done it. Hayley's face flushed as she realized what she had just said. "Let me climb. I don't have a fear of heights." That much was true, but scaling a cliff wasn't as simple as climbing a tree or a reaching the top of a playground. This was a matter of life or death.

Jack slowly edged his way back down. Hayley noticed his hands were shaking. "Don't do this," he told her. "It's too risky. You could die."

"One of us has to," she said. Her own words condemned her.

"We haven't got all day," Clyde snapped. "Get. Up. There."

With the color slowly returning to his face, Jack gripped Hayley's hand in an attempt to reassure her. "Just get high enough to see the clue."

She nodded. I can't believe I'm doing this. As soon as the men released her, she placed both hands on the cool stone and started climbing.

Chapter 25

The cliff face seemed larger than life as Hayley struggled onto the nearest ledge. In a matter of seconds, she was already breathing hard and wishing she hadn't taken Jack's place. *I'm a runner, not a rock climber.*

Every few feet she advanced, she looked up at the Tree of Death to see if she was making any progress. Its haunting features only taunted her, and she didn't dare look down to see how high she was above the camp.

"Hey, Cat Eyes!"

She shoved her toes against the stone gripped the ledge as hard as she could. "What?" she called, sneaking a glance over her shoulder.

"Catch!" It was Clyde. He tossed her a small black object. Hayley automatically reached out to grab it, forcing her body to lean back away from the cliff. A spike of fear jolted through her limbs. She quickly grabbed onto the ledge with her free hand, shuddering. That had been close—too close.

Fortunately, she had caught a string wrapped around the object between her fingers. She draped the string around her neck and glanced down. Binoculars.

Ten minutes later, Hayley had advanced only a third of the way up the cliff. Her fingers were stiff and sore from latching onto nooks and crannies. A cold sweat broke out on her forehead. She knew it only took one misstep for her to fall to her death—or end up with several broken bones. Or become paralyzed. Or—

Dang it, don't think like that, she scolded herself. Still gripping a ledge like her life depended on it, she looked up at the Three and groaned. It didn't look any closer than before.

She continued zigzagging up the cliff face, pausing constantly to plan her route and decide where to put her hands and feet. She never once looked down, though Clyde shouted at her every once in a while. She wondered what Jack was thinking. Was he worried sick? Was his heart pounding erratically in his chest, anticipating a slip or tumble? Once again, a rush of fear shot through Hayley's system, and she forced herself to continue.

She had no clue how she was going to get down. The thought had crossed her mind multiple times. She knew sometimes it was easier going up than it was going down. Midway up the cliff, she stopped on a large ledge and rested, trying to keep her thoughts focused on one thing and one thing only: the Tree.

"Easy, now," she told herself. With her feet firmly planted on the ledge, she continued to grip the cliff with one hand while grabbing the binoculars around her neck with her other. She fumbled for a moment, her fingers slipping on the string, before finally bringing the binocs to her eyes. She slowly raised her head and stared up at the Tree of Death, which was ringed with gold due to the rising sun. It gave the Tree an eerie orange glow.

Hayley realized her hand was shaking as she peered through the binocs. It took her about a minute to make the necessary adjustments to focus on the Tree. Once she did, she carefully panned from the top of the Tree to the bottom, studying all the intertwined branches.

"Do you see anything?" Clyde yelled.

"No!"

"Then go higher and keep looking!"

Those were the exact words she didn't want to hear. She was already so high up that one slip would mean certain death. How much higher did Clyde want her to go?

Instead of reaching for the next crevasse, Hayley stayed rooted to the spot and looked through the binoculars again. This time, she thought she saw something carved onto the bottom of the trunk. A hopeful smile grew on her face when she realized it resembled a triangle. Yes!

"I think I've got it!" she hollered. A chorus of whoops and cheers reached her ears. With trembling fingers, she slowly focused in on the faint triangle until she could make out the words written inside: l'eau.

Her smile disappeared. The word meant 'water' in English. Again? she thought hopelessly. Maybe when she and Jack closed their eyes, the accompanying clue would help narrow things down a bit. Or not.

She dropped the binocs and prepared to head back down. As soon as her free hand gripped onto the cliff face, one of her legs automatically stepped towards the ledge directly beneath her. The sudden shift in movement caused her foot to slide down a few inches. The ledge she had been standing on began to crumble. Before Hayley realized it, she was sliding down the face of the cliff, her hands frantically grabbing for something to hold onto. She screamed, her eyes wild with fear. The feeling of weightlessness made her heart jump into her throat. She was falling—falling to her death.

Chapter 26

As soon as Hayley's scream pierced the humid air, Jack felt like someone had stabbed him in the chest. He watched helplessly as her body tumbled down the cliff. "No!" he wanted to cry, but his mouth wouldn't cooperate. He was frozen in shock and horror.

Even Clyde seemed stunned. He cursed under his breath, though his frustration in no way mirrored Jack's. To him, Hayley was just a pawn. To Jack, she was...what? Hope? Beauty? Encouragement? With a painful cry, Jack realized just how much she meant to him. Before he knew it, his eyes pooled with tears.

Hayley's scream reverberated off the solid stone cliff. It was cut short when her hand snagged on one of the ledges. Her legs flailed for a few moments before she found her footing. The entire camp let out one collective sigh of relief.

"Hayley!" Jack yelled, sprinting forward. "Hold on! Are you okay?"

"I'm f-fine!" she called. She looked so small compared to the massive cliff. High above her, the Tree of Death loomed menacingly over her petite body. Judging by the streaks of dirt and small rocks still tumbling down, Hayley had slid a good fifteen feet. She stopped, clutching the ledge harder than before, and waited for a few minutes.

Jack could barely watch as she slowly worked her way down, ledge by ledge. She stumbled a few times, eliciting a few gasps and shouts of encouragement. Jack was surprised by how the men were reacting. They wanted her alive, of course, but judging by some of the worried expressions, they also cared for her. To a point.

Hayley took twice as long getting down as she did climbing up. Every movement was made with extreme caution. Jack knew her fingers must have been screaming in pain from such exertion. As soon as she touched the ground, he was the first to rush over to her. Even Clyde didn't pull them away when Jack wrapped his arms around her neck.

"Dang it, Hayley, I thought I'd lost you," he said.

She laughed nervously. "Not yet."

Jack thought he had never felt something as wonderful as her laughter vibrating against his chest. "You must be scraped up," he said, reluctantly pulling away.

"A little." She raised her arms for him to see, wincing when Jack touched her tender skin. She was bruised, scraped, and bleeding in multiple places, but she was still whole.

Clyde watched silently as Jack and another man, who had some rudimentary medical knowledge, tended to her needs. "That was quite a show," he said once they were done. "Good catch."

Hayley, still shaken up, couldn't even muster a glare. Jack did it for her.

"So what did you see?" Clyde asked greedily.

"L'eau. Water."

"Again?" he muttered.

Hayley looked away. Jack wished there was something else he could do for her.

"Well, what are you waiting for?" Clyde snapped. "Get the other half!"

Jack scowled. "Can't you give it a rest? She almost died."

"I don't care if she was beamed up by aliens. I'm on a schedule here. We need to find that treasure!"

"Fine," Hayley said, exasperated. She held Jack's hand with much less strength than she normally used. They closed their eyes. Clyde leaned forward eagerly, watching as different expressions flickered across their faces.

"My God," Jack murmured.

Clyde pounced. "What? What is it?"

"I can't believe this," Hayley said in an awed tone. She and Jack witnessed the brilliant light and jumble of symbols, as usual, but all the other clues paled in comparison to the one they now saw. It glistened and shone like a diamond. The words burned themselves into their minds.

"What?" Clyde said again.

Jack and Hayley opened their eyes and dropped their hands in unison. "Wow," she breathed. Jack whistled between his teeth.

Clyde, feeling left out of the loop, frowned and folded his arms across his chest. "This better be good."

Jack ignored him. "O-R," he spelled for Hayley.

It only took a fraction of a second for her to put the pieces together. "L'eau d'or," she murmured. "Golden water."

"Water? Water?" Clyde cried. "Of all the things...!" He swore and stormed away, causing Hayley to cringe. Jack instinctively placed a hand on her arm.

"Don't," she said when he opened his mouth to speak. "I know. I just need to ignore him."

"He should've learned by now that the clues aren't very specific. It's always by luck that we find them."

"Luck?" She turned to face him. "We're talking about a map that only we can see—one clue at a time—in our minds when we close our eyes and hold hands. How is that even rational? How is any of this rational? Why are triangles and words magically appearing all over the island, but only we can see them? It's like someone can see into our minds and reveal a part of the map to us bit by bit. It scares me." Her voice shook with fear. Jack wondered if she was simply strung up from her near-death fall, but the next thing she said slammed him with conviction.

"You act like you only know as much as I do, but I know better. You're hiding something from me." She narrowed her eyes. "You know what this map is."

Jack winced but remained silent.

"Whatever." Hayley bit her lip and walked away, ignoring the tendrils of hair that kept falling in front of her face. With her wild hairdo and soiled clothes, she looked just as rugged and exhausted as Jack did. "I need some time to think. I just want to get out of this crazy nightmare."

A reply was on the tip of Jack's tongue, but he restrained himself. *I've been living this 'crazy nightmare' for my entire life, Hayley. I wish I could explain it to you. Maybe someday*

I will. Here and now were obviously not the time and place, though.

Chapter 27

Both the sun and everyone's spirits were high by the time they left camp. Clyde was the only exception: he was in a sour mood that showed in everything he did. He swore, he kicked, he made a show of waving his gun around. Jack and Hayley, while staying out of each other's way, also tried to stay out of Clyde's. Though the men still treated Jack with contempt, they were a little nicer to Hayley after her near-death experience.

This wasn't the first time Jack felt a fool. He knew Hayley had showed him up by scaling the cliff. He was deathly afraid of heights, and now everybody knew it. He also didn't have a plan. As long as he was on this island, there was no chance of escaping. On the bright side, as long as Clyde didn't find the treasure, there was no chance of dying.

Jack wished there was some way he could come up with a red herring to throw Clyde off track. But there were two problems with that: he didn't know any French and Hayley wasn't speaking to him. He wrestled with his thoughts. Should I tell her...?

Jack had never told anyone his past. The only people who knew were his parents, and possibly one or both of them was dead. He frowned and poked the dirt with a stick. His bloodline was something he was ashamed of. He couldn't imagine explaining his history to anyone, even Hayley. If he told her, she wouldn't want anything to do with him.

He was so lost in his thoughts that he didn't hear the footsteps coming up behind him. Suddenly, a large hand grabbed the collar of his shirt and yanked him to his feet. "So, Nau, what's the plan?" Clyde spat.

Jack squirmed and fought to go free. Clyde let him go, but not before giving him a swift kick to the back. Jack sprawled onto the dirt.

"'Golden water,' eh? Where'd you come up with that one?" Clyde said.

"Sorry, that's all the clue said." Jack wiped his mouth and stood up, trying to ignore the white-hot pain spreading across his back.

"You're making this all up, aren't you?"

"I don't speak French."

"But your girlfriend does."

Jack ignored the girlfriend comment. "Why would we lie about something like this?" he argued. "How in the world would we make this up? Hayley just happened to be aboard the same ship as you and ran into me on the other island. Why on earth would we come up with such an elaborate plan when we're practically strangers?"

Clyde smiled evilly. "Because you're not strangers."

Jack was frustrated. "Just because we went to school together a long time ago doesn't mean we ever talked or made contact. We're strangers."

"You're trying to lead me away from the treasure. I know it. You're coming up with generic words and poorly-constructed clues in hopes that I won't find the loot." Clyde began pacing. "Well, you're wrong."

Jack rolled his eyes. The thought was so ridiculous he wouldn't reward the man with a reply.

"You need to know something about me, Jack. I'm not the kind of person you mess with. You've been cocky and sassed back to me this whole time. I can easily maroon you on another island—one with no freshwater and no means of survival."

And accomplish what? Killing off your link to finding the treasure?

"Or how about this? What if I tortured Cat Eyes over there?"

That got Jack's attention. His eyes snapped up and focused on Hayley, who sat in the shade holding a water bottle to her forehead. She had already gone through so much. Jack's stomach did a little flip. "You promised," he warned. "You can't touch her."

"We have to be nearing the end of this treasure hunt," Clyde said. "As soon as we get the last clue, I don't need you anymore. But why would I kill you when I can have the satisfaction of torturing your girlfriend first?"

Jack felt like throwing up. Clyde didn't need to know that the clue they just discovered—l'eau d'or—was, in fact, the final clue. Jack felt it in every cell of his being. The brilliance of the symbol in his mind's eye made him positive they were closing in on the treasure.

"The one thing that can break a man," Clyde continued, "is his weakness." He grinned, showing off a chipped tooth that Jack hadn't noticed before. "And it just so happens I know what your weakness is."

Jack swallowed. Don't look. Don't look. He squeezed his eyes shut, hoping they wouldn't betray him by wandering over to Hayley.

Clyde laughed maliciously. "I can break you, Nau. I can shut you down bit by bit until you're within an inch of your life. I can destroy you from the inside out, starting with her." He turned and whistled to the Spaniard, who was watching them intently. "Bring Cat Eyes over here," he ordered.

Jack's heart pounded in his chest when the Spaniard marched over to Hayley, grabbed her forearm, and hustled her to Clyde.

"Perfect," he purred. Jack was sickened. "You know I'm capable of doing what I say," Clyde continued. "I've hit you, beat you, threatened you, and abused you. I'm in charge. I'm the one with the power. You treat this like some sort of game, but I know you know better." He bent over so he was eye level with Jack. Lowering his voice, he said, "And believe me when I say this: once I get my hands on that treasure, you're going to wish you had never played these mind games with me. You're going to wish you had already died. You're going to wish Hayley had already died."

Jack narrowed his eyes. He imagined he could see into the man's soul. Past those dark, greedy pupils lay a vast emptiness, one that could never be filled. The hunger for power and wealth was insatiable. Jack was staring into the eyes of a madman.

Clyde grinned and backed away. "I hope I made myself clear."

"Crystal," Jack muttered, trying to appear unfazed while his heart hammered inside his chest. He willed himself not to peek at Hayley. Stay strong, he urged. Stay strong.

Clyde turned around and grabbed Hayley by her hair, eliciting a loud cry. "Boys," he shouted, "gather around! It's time to start looking for the Golden Water!"

Chapter 28

As expected, the l'eau d'or was harder to find than the Silver River, Spotted Rock, Water Grotto, and Tree of Death all thrown in together. The group spent the rest of the day and night walking the circumference of the island. They crossed the bay at twilight, and a few minutes later, they also crossed paths with the Silver River. Once they rounded the southeast tip of the island, they set up camp and decided to wait until morning.

Naturally, Jack and Hayley tried to stay as far away from Clyde as possible. Unfortunately, Clyde made it his personal duty to supervise them at all times. The last thing Hayley saw before she drifted off to sleep was the burly man's silhouette outlined by the crackling flames of their bonfire. Every few seconds, a sharp scraping sound could be heard thanks to Clyde whittling away at a rock with his knife. Hayley slept fitfully that night.

When she awoke, she was relieved to see Jack snoring softly across from her. She rubbed the sleep out of her eyes and sat up, wincing at the pain that shot down her back. When was the last time she had slept in a real bed? Would she ever get that luxury again?

Jack's guttural breathing was quickly swallowed by the other men's snores. Hayley frowned when she got to her feet. All around her were Clyde's goonies, sleeping the day away as if they had nothing better to do. Even the sentry, whose watch hours ended just after sunrise, was still asleep.

A gentle breeze reached Hayley's bare arms, and she shivered. Though her eyes were used to the hazy darkness, she spotted a thin arc of light rising from the east. The sun would rise within the hour.

Though her stomach growled and her throat was parched, Hayley needed to get away. She couldn't stand the sight of Clyde, and after her small falling-out with Jack, she could no longer confide in him. Despite their converging pasts, she knew she couldn't trust him until he explained what was going on. Secrets don't make friends, Jack, they make enemies.

As she zig-zagged her way through the sleeping camp, Hayley's thoughts drifted to her parents, and then to her Gran. She wondered what they would think of her now. "This wasn't my idea of an adventure," she whispered. "If I ever get home, I'll do my best to tell you all about it. Maybe then you'll realize I should have stayed in my apartment."

Suddenly, a loud boom erupted through the clearing, followed by a loud hissing and spraying of water. Hayley froze. What was that? It sounded like a bomb, gunshot, and stampede all at once, with a tidal wave thrown in.

Her skin crawling, Hayley glanced over her shoulder at the men. A few grunted in their sleep and turned over. The sentry continued to nod into his chest. Hayley briefly wondered if she should alert Jack, but when the sounds of the jungle continued as if nothing had happened, she relaxed. I'm just making a mountain out of a molehill. There's nothing to worry about.

Still on her guard, Hayley tiptoed through the jungle for a hundred yards until she reached the sand. Though the sun was still below the horizon, it was already humid. She pinched her tank top and waved it in and out, hoping to catch a breeze down her chest. As she tried to cool herself down, she glanced warily to her left and right, wondering where the source of the bomb/gunshot/stampede/tidal wave noise had come from.

There was nothing but sand and water in front of her, the jungle to her right, and tidepools to her left. She could even make out the Spotted Rock where it stood like a sentinel over the glittering sand. Everything looked completely normal—and beautiful, of course, in the early morning glow.

Hayley let go of her tank top and headed toward the tidepools. She sat down on a large rock overlooking the water and curled her knees up to her chest. Tears spontaneously sprang into her eyes. She cried silently as she watched the miniature sea life in front of her. How could there be so much life in a place of death? How could there be so much beauty, when all she saw was hate and greed?

She didn't know why she was crying, but it felt okay. She half-smiled at the bright sea stars, squishy sea anemones, and spiky urchins. Her fingers ached for her camera. Automatically, her brain switched tracks, reminding her of where she could have been at the moment—where she should have been. Gran's face came to mind, causing Hayley's tears to flow a little faster. She angrily wiped her face and stood up. Now was not the time to be daydreaming about what-ifs. She had to be in full survival mode, especially now that the treasure hunt was drawing to a close. A niggling thought in the back of her mind told her the only hope of survival was with Jack. They had to work together, whether they liked it or not.

Hayley folded her arms across her chest, blinking back tears as she squinted at the ocean. The sunrise was deceptively stunning. As far as she could see, the water was tinted with streaks of pink, yellow, and orange. Before long, the first arc of the sun rose above the horizon, forcing Hayley to shield her eyes from the glare. She half-expected a pod of dolphins to breach the surface of the water, their glossy backs illuminated by the piercing sunrise.

Instead, to her surprise she saw a section of the tide-pools begin to glow. She stood on her tiptoes and watched as it grew brighter and brighter. The rocks enclosing the five-foot tidepool sectioned it off from the rest, providing a sort of barrier. The rocks themselves seemed to reflect the brilliant sunrise onto the water. It reminded Hayley of swimming with the pool light on at night. The water was unnaturally tinted, but it was beautiful.

She had to get a closer look. Opting to take the long route along the edge of the pools, she hopped off her rock and jogged through the sand. Once she was close enough, she peered inquisitively into the illuminated depths. She realized the pool wasn't as shallow as she first thought. The bottom wasn't even visible.

As the sun continued to rise, the water only sufficed to glow brighter, until it shone with a golden hue that seemed fit for heaven itself. Hayley was stunned. What sort of natural phenomenon was this? The rocks were either glowing or reflecting the sun's light—either way, the shine produced was purer than anything Hayley had ever seen.

"Hey! What are you doing?"

Hayley snapped to attention. She saw Jack's silhouette standing on the edge of the foliage, one foot in the sand. "Hey!" he called again.

She pursed her lips. Should I...?

"What were you looking at?" Jack asked.

She caved. "You've got to see this! It's like gold water or something!"

"Gold water?" Jack yelled. "Are you serious?"

Hayley wrinkled her nose in confusion when Jack sprinted over. She didn't expect him to react so abruptly.

"Did you say gold water?" he cried breathlessly when he reached her.

"Um...yes?"

He grabbed her shoulders, his eyes glowing with excitement. "Holy crap, Hayley! Don't you realize what you're looking at?"

They both turned to stare at the illuminated tidepool. Hayley suddenly fell to her knees in shock. "Oh my gosh."

Jack whooped. "Gold water! You found it, Hayley!"

"I can't believe it," she whispered. Slowly, hesitantly, she reached out and touched the water. It was cool to her fingertips. She smiled.

"It's magic," Jack said, squatting next to her. He grinned and dipped his entire hand in the water. "Whoa."

"If I wasn't here watching the sunrise, I would have never found this."

"L'eau d'or," he said softly, the French words rolling awkwardly off his tongue. "Who would've known?"

"Apparently not Clyde and his men."

"They're still snoring away." Jack laughed.

"How did you wake up?"

"I slept horribly last night. I, um..." He paused awkwardly and scratched his head. A wave of guilt washed over Hayley. Thankfully, Jack plodded on. "It was one of those times when I kept slipping in and out of sleep. I was half-awake when I heard a loud crash."

"You heard it too?" Hayley had thought the noise was just a figment of her imagination. "I couldn't figure out what it was for the life of me."

"I didn't see anything. It made me jump right out of my sleep, though."

Hayley placed a hand on his arm. "Jack. Look—I'm sorry about what I said yesterday."

He glanced away from the glittering pool. "Don't be. You're right—you deserve some answers."

"Then tell me."

"It's a long story."

"I've got all the time in the world. Okay, so maybe only a half hour or so before the men start waking up."

Jack eased off the balls of his feet and sat down. His fingers weaved themselves into the coarse sand. "Wow...I've never really told anyone before. I haven't exactly had the best social life since high school."

"You can trust me," Hayley said quietly, sitting down as well.

"It's not trust that's the problem. It's actually getting the words out." Already Jack looked frustrated. "I don't even know where to start."

"Take your time. Just think about it." Hayley was itching to know what was going on. She couldn't believe Jack was actually going to tell her his story. Maybe it was the beautiful, calm atmosphere or the excitement over finding the last clue. But right now, the last thing Hayley wanted to do was hold hands and close her eyes. She was done with the map. She wanted to strategize, and that meant she needed answers.

Chapter 29

"I'm sorry, Hayley," Jack muttered. "I know what I want to say, but I don't know how to say it."

"It's fine." She squeezed his hand reassuringly. "Just start from the beginning."

He laughed dryly. "The 'beginning' is a lot earlier than you'd expect."

If Hayley was confused, she didn't show it. "Would it help if I told you my story?"

Jack glanced up in surprise. "Sure. It would help me collect my thoughts, at least."

"Okay." She smiled, but behind her vibrant green eyes lingered a definite sense of worry. "My story is probably much simpler than yours, since it starts in high school. I was almost done with my freshman year when I came home from school right in the middle of a major argument. My parents had fought a few times before, but they had never yelled or thrown things at each other until that moment."

Jack was horrified. "They threw things?"

"A pen, a book, things like that. It went both ways. I was scared, but the next morning everything was back to the way it was. I thought it had blown over. A few months later, they fought again, this time to the point where my mother threatened to move away from my father. It was an empty threat, of course, but in time I saw my father's work hours become longer and longer. My parents were drifting away. Sometimes I would come home from school to hear my mother crying in her bedroom with the door locked. I hated it.

"Sophomore and junior year were more of the same, but since neither of my parents talked about getting a divorce, I thought they were just going through a rough patch, and by keeping their distance they could live more peacefully with each other." She laughed dryly. "I was so naïve. I should have realized the peace was only temporary. After a while, my parents stopped talking to me so much. We hadn't eaten a meal as a family in years. But I was so caught up in my studies and friends that I didn't care. I tried to push it away—subconsciously, of course.

"From the outside, it looked like my family was picture-perfect. My dad was a little bit of a workaholic, and once my mom got a job, she started cranking out money too. The money was nice, I'll admit, but I was lacking the relationships I had as a child."

Jack nodded and realized Hayley was still gripping his hand. He didn't let go. "You always seemed so perfect in school. So..." Beautiful, he wanted to add, but he didn't dare.

"Maybe," Hayley said mysteriously, not looking his way. "I kept telling myself life was great. Things could be better, but things could be a lot worse, too. I had a ton of friends and people liked me. Not to brag, or anything." She grinned.

"Nah, it's the truth. You were popular."

"And a fat lot of good that did me," she snorted. "The only thing that remained from my time at Orange Grove was photography. My Gran gave me a camera in seventh grade, and it took off from there. All throughout high school I had my camera with me. I didn't realize it at the time, but taking pictures was like taking snapshots of memories. I could relive those memories whenever I wanted just with a click of a button."

Her tone suddenly grew remorseful. "The thing is, I don't have any pictures of my parents."

Jack swallowed.

"It shouldn't be a big deal, right? We didn't go on too many family vacations. We were drifting away when I was in high school. It made sense, but it still gets me to this day. Why don't I have any pictures of them?"

Neither wanted to voice the answer. Hayley plodded on. "Well, anyway, my life gets kind of crummy from here on. I'll keep it short to spare you."

"Don't," Jack said automatically. "Say whatever you're comfortable saying."

She nodded. "All right...well, senior year was good, I guess. I had more the same: friends, fun, photography, and a lack of family. I dated a few times, but I wasn't into it. As soon as I started thinking about college, boys took a backseat. I wasn't into the popularity as much. I mean, I was always thinking about college—it's like this giant obstacle in the back of your mind that you know you have to tackle, but you don't actually get around to tackling it until later. At least, that's how it was with me."

Jack nodded, even though he didn't really know what she was talking about.

"I dabbled around in different colleges, sent my applications, applied for scholarships, all that jazz. The first acceptance letter I received was from FIU, and that pretty much sealed the deal for me. I had grown up in Florida my whole life, and Florida International University seemed pretty sweet. My Gran lived nearby, I lived nearby, and that meant I was set for the next four years—or however long it would take for me to graduate. I wasn't interested in having a roommate or living in dorms. I was set in my ways."

She shook her head. "My naivety astounds me, even to this day. I should have seen it coming. As soon as I graduated from Orange Grove High, my parents got this funny look on their faces. Everything slipped into a sort of fantasy world. All my friends could talk about were college and boys and parties, which I wasn't really interested in, and I found myself drifting away from them as they packed up and moved out of state. I was alone except for my parents and Gran—and the former didn't really count. They had learned to live at peace with each other, but there weren't any strong ties to their relationship. Not anymore. As soon as they saw I was accepted into FIU, that sealed the deal."

"I'm sorry, Hayley," Jack murmured, already knowing what she was going to say next.

She nodded sadly. "Yeah...they moved away. They said they were 'transferred,' like their jobs were super demanding or something. It was like a punch to the gut. Why would they move all the way across the country, to L.A. of all places? Did Florida hold too many memories for them? Did they hate their only child so much that they had to leave her?"

Jack winced. Hayley's grip had become unbearably tight around his hand. Her eyes flashed with anger. "I don't think they hated you," he said softly. He placed two fingers on her chin and turned her head to face him. "Hey, listen to me. They didn't hate you. They created their own problems, and you weren't part of that. This was their fault. It had nothing to do with you."

"They saw they could get rid of me, so they did," she said bitterly.

"Are they still living together?"

She sighed. "No. I think they did in the beginning. I called every week the summer before college. Once I was bombarded with homework, I called every month. When I realized one of their numbers had changed and they stopped calling back frequently, I gave it a rest. We haven't talked in half a year, maybe."

"I'm sorry."

"I'm over it."

"I don't think you are, Hayley."

She squeezed her eyes shut. A few tears trickled down her cheeks. "You're right," she whispered.

"I'm guessing you're living the hateful dorm life, then?"

"No. My Gran still lives in Florida, so I'm staying with her. Well, next door to her, actually. She lives in a small apartment complex. It's only a 15-minute drive to the campus."

Jack nodded. "Things might work out, you know. Maybe your parents will realize what they missed as they get older."

"They'll never get back together."

"No, but they might come back to you."

Hayley let go of Jack's hand to wipe her eyes. "I hope so," she murmured.

Jack couldn't bear to see the hurt flickering across her features. As she shifted in the sand, silently wiping her tears, it took all of his self-control not to wrap his arms around her and hold her close.

"You know," she said quietly, "this is the first time in years that I actually miss them."

"Yeah, kidnapping can do that to you."

Jack was relieved when a smile broke out on her face. "I have to say, Jack Patterson, I think you're the best thing that's happened to me since I left on this boat trip."

He grinned. And you're the best thing that's happened to me as long as I can remember.

Chapter 30

It all made sense now—why Hayley had been so closed-off and shy in high school. She had been dealing with the turmoil of her parents' relationship for years. How could someone so beautiful and talented and popular keep that bottled up inside of her?

"Hey," she said suddenly. They had been sitting in the sand for a few minutes, studying the l'eau d'or in contemplative silence. The sunrise now illuminated sky and water with full force. The light was blindingly beautiful.

"It's your turn now," Hayley said.

Jack shifted uncomfortably. Yes, it was his turn. He had listened patiently when Hayley told her story. He couldn't believe what she had gone through. But boy, was she in for a surprise...

"Well, I've had some parent problems too, but of a different sort," he started lamely.

Hayley studied him carefully.

"You know what?" Jack laughed. "Let me start over. Um..."

"Start when you were a boy. What were your parents like? Where did you live?" Hayley suggested.

Oh, the memories that flooded in...

Jack shook his head to clear his thoughts. "Okay, I'll start there. At the beginning."

Hayley smiled reassuringly.

"My mom and dad were like normal parents, I guess. I was born and raised in Florida but moved all over. I don't remember where my birthplace was because we didn't stay in one place for more than a few months. That was my dad's fault. He worked for some online company, so he didn't have to 'go to work,' technically. We had a meager income my entire childhood. My mom worked odd jobs here and there, which helped a bit. Even though we moved a lot, it was usually between seedy apartments no more than 20-30 miles apart, so I was fortunate enough to be able to stay in the same elementary school.

"I didn't know better, of course. I was just a shy kid with two parents who I thought were the best parents in the world. My mom loved me to death, but my dad was a different story. He left when I was nine."

"I'm sorry," Hayley said quietly.

"Don't be. I hardly remember him at all. My mom didn't keep any pictures of him, so I can't even think about what his facial features look like. It doesn't matter. He's gone, and he was never really a part of my life."

Something in Jack's gut twisted, and he realized the irony of his statement. He cleared his throat. "Well," he corrected, "now that I think about it, my dad's been more a part of my life in the past few years than ever before."

Hayley was clearly puzzled. "Please explain."

"I'm getting there. It's still kind of confusing, sorting through the facts..."

She waited patiently while Jack furrowed his brow in concentration. He stared at the glittering golden water until he had gathered his thoughts. "After my dad left, I thought my mom and I were finally going to settle down. She needed to get a solid job. Dad's disappearance shook her so much that we had a hard time affording even our ramshackle apartment, which we were living in at the time. It was heartbreaking. I cried a few times because I'd always pictured my dad as this amazing guy. I loved him. I thought he had left me."

"He didn't?"

Jack shook his head. "My mom knew otherwise. Apparently she and my dad had been planning to leave the country for some time. We had moved around so much, not to find jobs and places with a roof over our heads, but to run away."

Hayley swallowed.

"I know it sounds crazy, but someone was after my dad. It took me nearly ten years to realize that. My mom never told me—she hardly told me anything; Dad's disappearance pretty much shut her up—but I figured it out anyway. I was only eleven when I found a crumpled piece of paper taped to the underside of my mom's...er...private drawer."

"I'm not going to ask what you were doing there."

Jack smiled sheepishly. "Actually, I was tracing this crack in the wall, and I pulled open the drawer not knowing what was inside."

"Underwear."

"Well, yeah...and other stuff too." His face reddened. "Anyway," he said swiftly, "since I was kneeling on the floor, I saw this slip of paper, and it seemed to have been put there on purpose. I ripped it off and read the small, 12-point type on the front.

"It was a newspaper article. Some of the words were blocked out, but I could read most of it. I didn't understand one bit. My mom had scribbled the word 'generations' on the top right corner, followed by a bunch of tally marks. I taped the paper back up and shrugged it off. My mom had some weird, piddle-y little habits, and I assumed this article was something she wanted to save for whatever reason."

"What did it say?"

"Fast forward a few years. I was an eighth grader, and for the first time in my life I used a computer."

Hayley grinned in spite of herself. "Nice."

"The librarian helped me use it to type some school papers. When I discovered Google, I had a legitimate lightbulb moment. I remembered the article I had found and typed in some of the words that came to mind. What I found was so horrible that it changed me. As cheesy as it sounds, it literally changed me from the inside out. I could never look at my father—or myself—the same way again."

Hayley leaned forward, listening intently.

"I didn't jump to conclusions right away. The process was slow and thought-provoking. I'll admit what I found was shocking, but it took me years to mull it over. I never told my mom what I had found."

"Which was...?"

"I'm getting to that."

"I hate when you keep me in suspense."

"Just listen. Okay, so now I'm in high school. Orange Grove was cool. I had a few friends—kind of. I was shy and un-athletic and socially awkward."

Hayley stifled a laugh. "I know."

Jack's face warmed. "That's when things started to change. The first few months of freshman year, everything clicked. I realized the immense danger I was in. What I had found in that article and later on Google finally made sense. It was horrifying. I became ashamed of who I was. I hated myself and my father—though I had a sense of respect for him for keeping our family safe."

Hayley held up a hand. "Whoa, back up for a second. You keep implying that your father didn't take off. Was he kidnapped? Who was after you?"

"He wasn't kidnapped. Well, technically, I don't know for sure. Most likely, he's dead."

She pursed her lips.

"That's not the worst part. The guys who took him and/or killed him didn't stop there. I knew they were after me, too. Because here's the thing." Jack leaned forward, his eyes wide open and glowing with the anticipation of what he was going to say next. "The tally marks my mom had made on that article were the number of generations. She knew my father's bloodline, and now I do too. The guys who were after my father knew I was alive. They were coming for me."

"I'm still confused, Jack."

"I'll explain everything in a second, don't worry."

"Wait—before you continue, let me get this straight," she said, frustrated. "So your dad has this big secret about why some guys are after him. They're also after you because of something in your bloodline. And whatever this secret is, your mom knows too, but she never told you. Why?"

Jack lowered his gaze. "It was shameful. My dad, and his dad, and his dad's dad, and hundreds of generations earlier—they were all ashamed. Because of this direct bloodline, we were under a curse."

Hayley raised an eyebrow.

"Oh, come on. You've seen the treasure map behind your own eyelids. Can't you believe in a curse?"

"Maybe. What's the curse?"

"It's in my blood." Jack nearly spit the word between his lips. His eyes darkened. "After I found out who I truly was, I hated myself. I hated the ocean. I hated the one man who started it all."

"Which was...?"

"A pirate."

"Whoa, your great-great-however many greats-granddad was a pirate?"

"It's not as awesome as it sounds," Jack muttered. "It's the worst thing that's ever happened to me."

"I still don't understand how that's a curse. Why would your mom keep that from you? Why would someone be after your dad—and you, too?"

Jack sighed. "Hayley, don't you get it? I have a map. I have a treasure map in my freaking mind that no one else can get to. If I was born with this map, that means my dad probably was too, and so on. Everyone in my ancestor's direct bloodline had the map.

"Why else would a gang kidnap my dad and (most likely) kill him? It's the same thing Clyde's doing to me now. The bad guys want the treasure, and to find the treasure they need the map. I have the map. And for some reason, you just happen to be caught in this mess."

Hayley didn't reply. She stared at the golden water, which was now fading back to its normal cerulean hue. The tide was rising, covering the tips of the rocks that surrounded the golden pool. "I get it," she said softly. "I get it, Jack. I'm so sorry about what you've gone through. I'm amazed at your mom for carrying you through all of it."

"She's gone," he said quickly.

"What?"

"My mom's not in my life anymore. I don't know where she is or if she's still alive."

"Oh, Jack..."

He shook his head. "The last two years of high school, I realized someone was onto me. It might have been the same men who took my father, or it might have been a different group. I knew I had to get away.

"After high school, I finally broke down and told my mom everything. She was surprised, but a little relieved that I had figured it out. She didn't have much to add, except for the fact that she had kept her maiden name, Patterson, in hopes that we wouldn't be linked to my ancestor."

"Patterson's not your real last name?"

"No." Instead of going into details—to Hayley's annoyance—Jack cleared his throat and continued. "That was the last time I saw my mom. After that, I was on the run. College wasn't even an option. I took off to put distance between us. I didn't want my mom to get caught in the middle of this—like you are, unfortunately. I took to wandering the streets, working a few odd jobs, creating aliases, and looking over my shoulder at every turn.

"You can see what the life of a runaway did to me," Jack said sheepishly. "I worked out in my free time when I wasn't scavenging for food and water. I was tailed quite a few times, but I managed to elude the guys who were after me. I made my way south, planning to head to the Keys, despite my hatred of the ocean. No matter how badly I wanted to go home, get my mom, and move across the country, I couldn't. I was broke and utterly lost. My life had become that of a criminal's, even though I had committed no crime."

Hayley remained silent. Jack plunged his hands into the sand and squeezed the grains between his fingers, fuming. The "lost years," as he liked to call them, were still vividly engrained in his mind.

"And then Clyde found you," Hayley said suddenly.

Jack nodded.

"You never heard from your mom? Do you think she's still living where you last saw her?"

"I don't know. Maybe someone knew she was a link to me. She could have been used. Clyde might have gotten information from her, which helped him find me." Each syllable sounded strained, as if it was a struggle to form the words. "I don't know," he repeated helplessly.

Hayley and Jack locked eyes. Despite the natural beauty surrounding them, both knew they had to get away from this place. They didn't care that the l'eau d'or was the final clue. An awkward silence had ensued, and each needed their time to think.

"Look," Hayley said, "before we go, we should talk strategy. Obviously, we can't let Clyde find the treasure."

"I can't do this right now." Jack closed his eyes and let out a sigh. He was emotionally and mentally drained. "I'm spent, Hayley. I'm sorry."

She pursed her lips. "I understand." She stood up and brushed the sand from her legs and shorts. "Do you mind answering one last question?"

He nodded wearily. "Shoot."

"Who was your pirate ancestor, exactly?"

Jack groaned. Of all the questions...

Before he even had a chance to reply, a roar came from the jungle behind them. They turned to see Clyde and the Spaniard storming across the sand, a murderous glint in their eyes.

"I guess we'll have to put a pin in it, then."

Hayley smiled weakly at Jack's mild humor, all the while bracing herself for what was to come.

Chapter 31

"Get them!" Clyde yelled.

Jack, who was seated in the warm sand, leaped to his feet and stepped protectively in front of Hayley. He willed his thoughts to return to survival mode. Now was not the time to dwell on the past, which he had spilled to Hayley just moments earlier. He had to act in the present.

The Spaniard was the first to reach them. Since he was much larger and stronger than Jack, he easily overpowered the youth and sent him sprawling on the sand. Jack's head landed dangerously close to a rock.

Hayley, who had been watching wide-eyed, took a few tentative steps backward.

"Get her!" Clyde screamed. "What are you waiting for?"

The Spaniard lunged forward and grabbed Hayley by the waist. He spun her around and pulled her wrists together behind her back, nearly dislocating her arms. She cried out in pain.

Jack jumped up and launched himself at the Spaniard, but Clyde was quick enough to grab him just in time. Now both men held their victims hostage, grinning evilly. "You still think you can outmatch us, don't you, Nau?" Clyde spat.

In reply, Jack twisted his hips and jabbed Clyde in the jawbone with his elbow. The man automatically released his grip and clutched his jaw. Hayley struggled to free herself as well, but the Spaniard was pure muscle and grit. She succeeded in kicking him in the shins, but it was to no avail. Even Jack, who succeeded in planting another hit to Clyde's face, was forced to give up.

The silhouettes of three men appeared at the fringe of the jungle. Now hopelessly outnumbered, Jack and Hayley ceased their efforts. They were trapped once again.

Hayley brushed some loose, tangled strands of hair out of her eyes. She spread her feet apart and rested her hands on her knees, panting. She could feel sand stinging her eyes and coating her limbs. She felt filthy, hungry, and sapped of all strength. When was it going to end?

"Who was on sentry duty?" Clyde snapped.

"Billings, sir," one of the men replied.

Clyde cursed. "Bring him to me," he ordered, before turning his attention back to Jack and Hayley. "As for you two, if you don't tell me where this 'golden water' is within the next half-minute, the deal's off." He glared at Jack. "Cat Eyes goes first."

Before Clyde could even pull out his gun, Jack spoke. His voice was calm and controlled, though hindered somewhat by his labored breathing. He wiped his sweaty forehead and said, "I know."

"You know what?"

"Where the golden water is."

Clyde's countenance softened slightly. He started at the sudden turn of events. "And?"

"It's right under our noses." Jack turned and gestured theatrically towards the tidepools, which were now almost entirely covered by the rising tide. "It's not exactly golden anymore, though. The sunrise tints the water color."

Hayley gaped at him. "Jack!" she wanted to cry. "What on earth are you doing?" She bit her tongue, forcing herself to remain silent. What was Jack's leverage? Why would he so willingly give away the last clue's location?

Clyde bounded forward, spurred on by greed. "Where's the treasure? Where is it?"

"I don't know," Jack admitted.

"What do you mean, you don't know?"

He shrugged.

As if some imaginary switch had been flipped, Clyde snapped back into an enraged fervor. "You're trying my patience, Nau!" He raised a fist as if to strike Jack, but Hayley cried out.

"It's over here!" She splashed into the tidepool surrounded by rocks, nearly twisting her ankle in her haste. "The treasure should be here. The water was golden at sunrise."

Clyde shoved Jack aside and made a beeline for Hayley. His lackeys were right behind him. Hayley suddenly found five greedy pairs of eyes staring at her as if she was an object of consumption. She gulped.

"Show me," Clyde demanded. When Hayley didn't respond right away, he added, "Now!"

She flinched and waded into the center of the tidepool. "There's a t-tunnel," she stammered. "Jack and I didn't get a chance to explore it. Maybe the treasure's in there."

Clyde splashed into the pool and stopped next to her, peering at the rocky, underwater tunnel. "Interesting," he said. As Hayley watched him, she imagined the gears in his head starting to turn. He suddenly reached out and grabbed her arm. "You're coming with me," he growled. He splashed noisily out of the tidepool with Hayley stumbling behind him. Once they were back on the sand, he motioned for Jack to come forward.

Despite the defiant glare in his eyes, Hayley could tell Jack was afraid. They had finally reached the last clue, and neither knew what Clyde was going to do next.

"Nau!" Clyde snapped. "You're going to swim through that tunnel, find the treasure, and swim back out."

"What if the treasure's not there?" Jack replied, crossing his arms over his chest.

The Spaniard lunged forward and backhanded him. "Shut up and listen," he ordered.

Clyde smiled approvingly. "You better hope the treasure's there." He gripped Hayley's arm tighter, and she bit back a painful cry. "If you don't resurface, or if you don't come back with some sort of evidence, you can say goodbye to our little deal."

Jack's eyes narrowed.

"If you come back with good news, the girl lives. If you come back empty-handed—or don't come back at all..." He grinned evilly.

"Play it smart, Jack," Hayley said. "You don't know where the tunnel goes. What if you run out of air?"

Clyde shoved her to the ground. "Shut up."

Jack started, but the Spaniard raised his fist in a warning. Hayley struggled to her feet, brushing the sand from her face and arms. She nodded. You can do this.

"Well?" Clyde snapped.

Jack clenched and unclenched his fists. "Yeah, yeah. I'm going."

The air was tense and silent as Jack waded into the tide-pool. Hayley knew Clyde was just using him as a guinea pig to find the treasure, and she was the bait. She had always been the bait. Almost unwillingly, Jack seemed to care for her. Clyde loved using it to his advantage.

"Be safe," she whispered, watching as Jack took a deep breath and dipped underwater. The pool was so shallow that his legs stuck out for a few seconds. He floundered, then disappeared into the tunnel, leaving only a few splashes in his wake.

Chapter 32

T hough he hated to admit it, Oliver was panicking. It had been nine days since he had last seen Hayley. He had searched far and wide for her on The Queen Francis, but the rumors had proved true—Hayley Slade was missing. Along with her, a group of men had disappeared as well. It was a scandalous affair that nearly proved the ruin of Queen Floridian Boat Tours. Though they tried to keep it hush-hush, the media quickly became involved, bloating the thing to a full-scale kidnapping and possibly murder.

Oliver was sick with grief. His spring break was meant to be relaxing and fun, but those seven days had passed in worry and fear instead. Now, on the first Friday after school had resumed, he was still agitated. Where could Hayley be? What was her connection to those men? His thoughts ran away with all sorts of unpleasant scenarios. It took an overwhelming amount of self-control to force himself to stick to the facts.

As he walked towards the student parking lot on FIU's campus, twirling his phone between his fingers, it reminded him of the last time he'd spoken to Hayley. You're a stuttering fool, his thoughts told him. You're nothing more than a failure. Look at yourself—you knew something was wrong and you had a chance to save Hayley, but you didn't! She might be dead because of you!

He squeezed his eyes shut and crawled into his car. "No," he murmured. "I tried to save her. I thought she had made it back to the boat. I thought she was okay."

You didn't think hard enough!

The accusing voices suddenly ceased when Oliver scrolled through his contacts and paused on Hayley's number. Her digits flashed through his mind like white-hot Christmas lights. In a triumphant lightbulb moment, he realized what he had to do. Though he didn't have the brawn and wits that made guys his age appealing, he did have his brain.

Oliver sped out of the parking lot. He could find Hayley. He knew it. The solution was right at his fingertips—literally.

Chapter 33

An odd sense of déjà-vu hit Jack as soon as he ducked inside the tunnel. Was it really only a few days ago that he had swam inside a similar tunnel, only to find the beautiful grotte d'eau? Now he was looking for treasure—what kind of treasure, he didn't know—that might or might not have been placed here. For all he knew, he could be wasting his time.

To his frustration, the tunnel didn't widen as it made its slow descent under the tidepools. Jack's sense of direction told him he was heading towards the sea, but would the tunnel eventually empty into the ocean, or would he reach a dead end? He had already been underwater for thirty seconds. Just fifteen or twenty more, and he would have to turn around and work his way back to the surface.

As the water around him grew darker and the tunnel walls became slick with moss, Jack suddenly realized the tunnel was getting wider, contrary to his expetations. He smiled, his nerves tingling with excitement. He was so close. He imagined discovering another grotto, this time filled with the exploits of his pirate ancestor—an underwater treasure chest.

But that wasn't the case. Though the tunnel did widen considerably, it merely emptied into a large cave that sloped towards the ocean. Jack could tell by the slow current that the tides caused the water to ebb back and forth. However, there was no treasure in sight—and more importantly, nowhere to resurface.

Jack turned around, defeat crushing his spirit like a ton of bricks. He had failed. Unless he used his wits to save Hayley, she was a goner. *Think, man! There's gotta be a way out of this!*

He scanned the large underwater cave one last time. There was nothing but golden sand and brown-gray rock as far as he could see. The current slowly pulled him away from the tunnel and into the center of the cave, and that's when he saw it.

There was another way out. Jack shouted in triumph, then quickly closed his mouth after a torrent of air bubbles streamed between his lips. He scissor-kicked over to the second tunnel, which was much larger than the one that came from the tidepool. To his relief, the passage widened out into a shallow pool. He broke the surface and gulped in precious air. Once his lungs were no longer burning, he took in his surroundings.

The pool was about four feet deep and eight feet in diameter. Directly above him, a narrow opening let in rays of sunlight. Jack stood in the center of the rocky pool, grateful for the golden hue that lit the cave.

But 'cave' didn't seem to be the right word. Jack frowned. The edges of the rock became more jagged—pointed, even—as they converged towards the narrow opening at the top. The lower portion of the walls were streamlined and smooth.

Just then, Jack realized a faint gurgling noise was coming from behind him. He turned around and saw the water ebbing and flowing along the entrance. Whenever it pulled away, it sucked at the rock and created a wet gurgling sound. As Jack studied the ebb and flow of the tide, he realized it was steadily rising. Before long, the entire pool would be flooded with water.

Since his heart was still beating at a rapid pace, Jack decided to wait another minute or so and catch his breath. To his surprise, though the water in the pool was indeed rising, it suddenly dipped back down to its original level, leaving a loud smacking gurgle in its wake.

What the...?

Jack's brow creased in confusion. For a split second, his thoughts were anywhere but on finding the treasure and saving Hayley. He knew the ebb and flow of water, this strange pool, the narrow opening at the top, and the loud explosion/gunshot noise he had heard earlier were all linked. The dots were there; he just had to connect them.

The solution suddenly came to him—he wasn't in any ordinary pool. He wasn't even in an ordinary cave. He was in a blowhole.

Grinning with the success of his discovery, Jack stared in fascination at the opening directly above his head. It all made sense. He couldn't wait to tell Hayley.

Crap—Hayley! His sense of excitement quickly ebbed away like the water around him. He sucked in a huge breath of air and dove back under. When he swam back into the large underwater cave that connected the two tunnels, he spotted something out of the corner of his eye. Buried partly in the sand were two glimmering points of light.

Jack paused, and his body automatically began floating upwards. He clung to the wall to keep himself from rising. With one hand, he scooped his fingers into the sand and came up with two tarnished, but otherwise perfectly shaped, coins.

No way.

Those were the only thoughts running through his head as he gaped at the coins. His heart pounded wildly in his chest. He couldn't believe it. A shiver of delight ran from his fingers to the rest of his body. No way!

Other than their tarnished surfaces, the coins were in mint condition. Jack turned them between his fingers, unwilling to believe what he was seeing. This couldn't be real. After all he and Hayley had been through, could the treasure actually still exist? Could it be somewhere inside this underwater cave? Could it even be right under his fingertips?

Jack wasted no more time. He stuck the two coins in his pocket and began digging. As sand mushroomed around him, floating lazily upwards, he came up with four more coins. These were also in excellent condition, with strange markings and various sizes and hues. It was amazing. To his dismay, Jack could not find anything else. He stuck the coins in his pocket and resurfaced in the pool, then dove underwater again. He dug throughout the entirety of the cave, but came up empty-handed each time. His movements became slower and less enthusiastic. Were these six coins the only evidence of his ancestor's treasure? Was that all?

There has to be more, Jack thought, disappointed. There has to be. But the more he searched, the more he proved himself wrong.

He resurfaced in the pool one last time. Amazement and excitement had quickly dissolved into frustration. Oh, well. Clyde had asked for evidence, and evidence is what he would get. It seemed like the rest of the treasure was gone.

That's when Jack heard it—another loud smack, followed by a strange gurgle, and then something terribly unexpected: a rumble. It seemed like the wall across from him was shaking. Was this some sort of underwater earthquake?

Before Jack could react, he saw the sand at the opposite side of the underwater cave suddenly begin draining away. The water became murky with all the particles floating around. A few seconds later, the rumbling stopped.

Jack tentatively swam forward. A strong current, which hadn't been there before, pulled him towards the narrow opening that had suddenly appeared at the base of the cave. Sand and water were sucked through, creating a miniature whirlpool. Fortunately, Jack was too big to fit through the six-inch-wide hole. He watched in fascination as the current grew stronger and stronger. The water in the pool was draining at an extremely fast rate. All of a sudden, it slowed again, creating a miniature dam of sand that blocked the small hole.

Jack was amazed. Did the water displacement somehow affect this little hole? Was it like some sort of drainage system for the bigger blowhole, which was on the opposite side of the cave?

That's it! His mouth dropped open in shock, releasing another torrent of air bubbles. He quickly swam over to the pool and resurfaced. Water droplets poured from his hair and skin. A drainage system...

The blowhole and miniature current worked as opposites. While the blowhole spouted water, the smaller hole drained sand—and treasure. Jack figured he had only found six coins because the rest of the treasure had been sucked through the hole. He rubbed his eyes, unaccustomed to this overload of information.

The next question, then, was where did the treasure go? Did the hole lead to open ocean, or to another cave? Jack realized with a stab of guilt that he had gotten so caught up in his excitement that he had completely forgotten about Hayley.

No! He squeezed his eyes shut and prayed for her life. He had wasted too much time in this strange connection of tunnels and caves. For all he knew, Clyde believed Jack to have drowned and already shot Hayley. Jack needed to get back to the surface.

With the coins still jangling in the pocket of his jeans, Jack dove underwater and swam to the original tunnel. In his haste, he scraped his shoulders against the rocky sides. But that was only the least of his worries. Panic quickly settled in. Please let her be alive. Please let her be alive!

Once the bottom was shallow enough to stand, Jack forced himself through the opening of the tunnel and stumbled to his feet. He was back in the tidepool. With a loud cry, he announced, "Wait! I found it!"

But it was too late. The first noise he heard was the deafening echo of a gunshot across the beach.

Chapter 34

Hayley, sick with worry and riddled with fear, stood directly in front of Clyde with his gun shoved in the small of her back. She stood this way for what seemed like hours, wondering where on earth Jack could be. When the men started to grow restless, she forced herself not to cry. Jack's still alive. He must have found the treasure.

But as the minutes ticked by, she realized she had to confront her worst fears. She wondered if being shot hurt as much as movies portrayed it to be. Maybe she wouldn't even hear the sound. Maybe there would be a sudden flash of pain, and then nothing.

As these thoughts plagued Hayley's mind, Clyde and his men suddenly shifted their attention from the tidepool to the two silhouettes marching towards them. As the pair came into view, Hayley realized it was the Spaniard and Billings.

Much to her relief, Clyde withdrew his gun from her back. "Billings!" he roared.

The man, just as large as Clyde, gritted his teeth and set his jaw. He knew what was coming.

"Were you not on sentry duty?" Clyde demanded.

"I was."

"Then why didn't you see our two hostages sneaking out of the camp?"

Billings shifted his weight from one foot to the other. "I—I was asleep."

Clyde pointed his gun straight at the man. "You were asleep."

"I'm sorry, sir. It won't happen ag—"

But Billings never got to finish his sentence. Clyde pulled the trigger, and Billings' body went limp. He crumpled to the sand, never to rise again.

Hayley didn't scream. She simply couldn't. She wasn't even able to will herself to move. She was absolutely stunned. Her eyes were focused on the bright red circle bleeding through Billings' shirt. Oh, God...

"Hayley!" a voice suddenly exclaimed. Everyone turned around and dropped open their mouths in shock at the sight of Jack, dripping wet, standing in the middle of the tidepool.

"You're back!" Hayley cried, her feet suddenly able to move. She attempted to rush forward, but Clyde grabbed her and held her back.

Jack's wild look slowly dissolved when he realized Hayley was alive and in one piece. "You're okay?" he asked. "I thought—"

"I shot Billings, Nau, not your girlfriend," Clyde spat. "But don't worry, she's next on my list."

"Don't!" Jack cried. He stumbled out of the tidepool and rushed forward. "Look! It's down there! I found the treasure!"

The murmuring of a dozen voices filled the air as the men crowded around Jack and Clyde. Jack dug his hand into his pocket and presented the evidence—six golden, gleaming coins.

The effect was instantaneous. Excitement and greed quickly replaced the bloodthirsty look in the men's eyes. Clyde snatched the coins from Jack and ran them eagerly between his fingers. "Well, well," he murmured. "Boys, look what we've found—the treasure."

The men whooped. "After all these years of searching," Clyde said, "we finally have it! We'll be rich, boys!"

Jack and Hayley were caught up in the fray as the men stampeded forward, crushing the delicate sea life in the tide-pool. The tunnel was barely wide enough for the men to fit, but Hayley knew a tight squeeze wasn't going to stop them. They were consumed by greed.

Surprisingly, Clyde was at the back of the pack. He clutched the gold coins like they were his lifeline, but he gripped his two hostages even tighter. "You're coming with us," he ordered, shoving them towards the tunnel. As soon as the last man had forced his way inside, Hayley knelt and took a deep breath.

"It's not that far," Jack said. "You can make it."

She nodded, convinced. True to his word, the tunnel wasn't really that long. She figured she had twenty more seconds of air by the time she reached the underwater cave. As she floated, wondering where the rest of the men had gone, she realized there was another tunnel on the opposite side of the cave. She quickly swam in that direction and broke through the surface. All around her, the men were marveling at the small pool and drinking in precious oxygen.

Up above, a small opening let in rays of sunlight. It was fringed by a serious of sharp spikes and rough-hewn rock. Hayley shivered.

Jack and Clyde surfaced last. With so many bodies in one spot, it was a tight fit. Hayley found she couldn't even move an inch to the right or left. The air in the pool, though it soothed her burning lungs, was moist and cold.

"So where is it?" one of the men demanded. "Where's the treasure?"

"I'll show you," Jack said. Hayley noticed his eyes were flickering around the pool. He looked uncharacteristically nervous about something. That was when Hayley realized the water level was falling and rising. The ebb and flow of the tide was strangely fast. What was going on?

"This might sound strange, but there was a current flowing from this pool towards the other side of the cave," Jack explained slowly. "It pulled some sand and water beneath the cave wall, but the hole was only six inches wide. I didn't see where the current led, but I'm assuming it's to the ocean."

"You're saying the rest of the treasure was sucked out?" Clyde asked.

"Exactly."

The men were both puzzled and surprised. "So where do we go?" one asked.

"This way," Jack said, edging towards the entrance of the tunnel. He gave a pointed look at Hayley before diving underwater. She took his signal to mean something's up. Her adrenaline levels spiked.

Thanks to the greedy men, she was shoved forward and forced to take a breath to dive back underwater. Everyone rushed after Jack, swimming and kicking in a mass of tangled limbs. Hayley's lithe figure managed to squeeze out of the middle of the pack and cling to one of the cave walls. She watched, her air supply slowly running out, as Jack gestured to the bottom of the wall. There was a small pileup of sand at the base, which she assumed was blocking the hole that Jack had described earlier. Interesting.

Jack pushed off the wall and floated towards Hayley, allowing Clyde and the men to get a better look. They began digging at the sand until the hole reopened. Jack turned to face Hayley, his eyes wide.

She cocked her head, as if to say, "What's wrong?"

He just nodded and grabbed her wrist. With his other hand, he pointed towards the original tunnel that led back to the tidepool. "Go," his eyes seemed to say. "And hurry!"

Hayley swam towards the tunnel, unsure of what Jack was doing. Were they seriously going to try to escape? There was nowhere to go once they were back on shore. Clyde still had a few men on the Antonia, and the island was so far away from shipping lanes that they would never be discovered. What could Jack possibly be thinking?

He pushed her. "Go!" his eyes urged.

Hayley nodded and ducked inside the tunnel. Jack let go of her wrist. She peeked over her shoulder to see if he was following her, and smiled when she realized he was. Behind him, Clyde and his men were swimming around the hole and marveling at the current it produced. They kicked and shoved, frantic with greed.

But something was wrong. Hadn't Jack said the current flowed out of the hole? If so, why was it suddenly flooding in? The small pool would be filled with water, and then the men would have nowhere to resurface to breathe. Even Hayley's lungs were already burning, and she was only a quarter way up the tunnel.

Jack pushed her forward, and she continued swimming. Whatever was happening, Jack wanted them to get out of there, and fast.

The farther Hayley went, the narrower the tunnel became, until she couldn't look over her shoulder to see what was going on. She hoped Jack was still behind her. His touch was no longer on her back, shoving her forward.

Suddenly, a slight current started to slow her process. She was almost at the tidepool, but the current only grew faster and faster. Water rushed in at alarming rates.

It took all of Hayley's efforts to break the surface and not get sucked back under. As she gulped in air, she clung to the rocks at the side of the tidepool. The current was so strong that if she let go, there was no doubt she would be swept under.

Where was Jack?

That was the only question in her mind as she watched the strange current. It was then that she realized the tide had risen so high that the water from the other tidepools was pooling into this one. All the excess water was creating the deadly current.

"Jack!" Hayley cried, hanging on for dear life. "Oh, God..."

But the current was so strong that it was impossible he could resurface. Tears streaked down her cheeks as Hayley realized he had probably been swept back into the underwater cave. No...

Suddenly, in a tremendous explosion of water, the sound of a gunshot reached her ears. A magnificent plume of water shot into view. It easily reached seventy or eighty feet before crashing back onto the rocks. The sound was like a gunshot, explosion, and stampede all mixed into one.

It was a blowhole. Hayley quickly made the connection and realized it was the same sound she had heard earlier that morning. Her revelation was crushed when she saw the water shooting from the blowhole suddenly turn a dark red. A chill ran down her spine.

As blood and water splattered onto the rocks, Hayley knew she was going to be sick. Only when the blowhole ceased spouting, and the current in the tidepool stopped flowing, did she stumble onto the sand and throw her head between her knees. She threw up was little was left in her stomach. Just one word continued to pound in her head.

Jack...Jack...

Chapter 35

B attered and bruised, Hayley curled up on the sand and cried. She was hungry, thirsty, exhausted, and—most of all—grief-stricken. She lay on the beach for what seemed like hours. The merciless sun beat down on her skin until she was as red as a tomato. Her clothes, skin, and hair quickly dried. Yet she continued to cry until there were no tears left.

So much had happened since she had first set foot on The Queen Francis. In just twelve days, she had explored deserted islands, cruised through the Caribbean, gotten kidnapped by a greedy gang of treasure-hunters, and experienced things she had never experienced before—namely, having part of a treasure map inside her mind. The fact that her one lifeline, Jack Patterson, was suddenly gone, made it unbearable. How would she ever return home? How would she see Gran again? Heck, if her parents miraculously showed up and rescued her, she would take back every spiteful thing she had ever said about them.

Hayley wiped her eyes and ran her fingers over her puffy, chapped lips. She needed water and food. It wouldn't do her any good to bake in the hot sun, mourning her losses.

Reluctantly, she stood up on shaky legs. Her joints groaned as she stretched to her full height. Tangled wisps of hair flew in front of her eyes as she trudged back towards camp. She didn't dare look back at the glittering tidepools—she hated them with a passion. In fact, she hated the whole island. She never wanted to see another island as long as she lived.

The jungle greeted her with its usual sticky humidity, vibrant green foliage, and buzzing insects. Hayley paused down in the middle of the clearing, looking around her at what was left of the camp. Bags and backpacks were strewn everywhere. The remains of last night's bonfire popped and sizzled, emitting a smoky odor that caused Hayley to wrinkle her nose.

Her primordial urge for food quickly took over, and she rummaged through the men's backpacks until she found a sandwich and half-empty bottle of water. The water was warm, but as it ran down her swollen throat it felt like the most refreshing draught she had ever taken. Once she was done with her meager dinner, she curled up on top of a few bags and stared up at the now-darkening sky. Though she didn't want to think about it, she knew she had to come up with a plan. She was stuck here forever, unless she somehow contacted a passing ship or the Coast Guard came looking for her. She could only imagine what Gran was feeling. Did her parents even know?

Suddenly, Hayley realized another dilemma: three of Clyde's men were still on his boat anchored in the bay. How long would it be before they came ashore, wondering where their leader went? Or would they simply give up on the treasure and leave? Either way, Hayley was doomed. She figured her best chance of staying alive was to remain on the island and live off whatever it produced, like Jack had done for six months.

At the thought of Jack, her gut twisted, and she squeezed her eyes shut to fend off tears. Maybe it was because his death was so sudden, or maybe because he was closer to her than any friend had been, but she missed his presence more than she missed Gran.

As the scorching sun gave way to twilight, and twilight gave way to the inky blackness of night, Hayley cried herself to sleep.

Hayley was grateful neither the sunrise nor the loud boom of the blowhole woke her. She merely roused to nature's call. After doing her business behind a palm tree, she pushed her emotions away and forced herself to get down to business.

First things were first: she needed breakfast. That brought to mind the few backpacks that were left by the tidepools yesterday. Not wanting all the food, water, and belongings to spoil, she trekked through the jungle and onto the beach. She frowned at the Spotted Rock and glared at the tidepools when they came into view. Once she reached the area where Clyde's men had left their backpacks, a foul odor suddenly reached her nose.

She froze and took a few steps backward. What in the world was that awful smell?

Holding her tank top over her nose, Hayley inched forward until she spotted Billings' corpse lying behind a rock. She shuddered and averted her eyes, but her brain had already taken a mental picture. Maggots and fleas had visited the body overnight.

Hayley tried to ignore the smell as she gathered whatever she could carry—namely, four huge backpacks. She kept her gaze downward as to not look at the tidepools. Don't think about him. Just don't.

Once she had returned to the clearing, she set the backpacks down and rested her aching shoulders. She was still in the process of stretching when the crackling of a radio startled her.

She glanced left and right. The noise seemed to be coming from the spot where Clyde had slept two nights ago. She crawled over and rummaged through his bag until she found his radio. As she held it in her hand, a man's voice suddenly came over the speakers: Sir, this is Vasquez. I repeat, this is Vasquez. You wanted us to contact you 5 days after we dropped anchor. The crackling stopped.

Hayley was frozen with fear. "Uh-oh," she muttered.

After a few minutes, the radio crackled to life again. I repeat, this is Vasquez. You wanted us to contact you 5 days after we dropped anchor. This is an emergency—an unmanned boat has been spotted in the bay. I repeat, this is an emergency!

Hayley shoved the radio back into Clyde's bag. Great. Now she had three more men to deal with, and a mysterious unmanned boat. Her heart rate automatically picked up. Was someone coming to rescue her?

Jack would know what to do, she thought. He would have a plan. He would even laugh about how worried I am right now. She smiled for a fraction of a second. A pair of tears ran down her cheeks. She could stay strong without him. She had to.

The radio crackled sporadically throughout the day, sometimes with Vasquez's voice and sometimes with another man's. Each time, Hayley felt a shiver of dread run down her spine. Finally, just before sundown, one last message was delivered: Sir, me and the boys are gettin' worried. We're comin' ashore first thing tomorrow morning unless we hear back from you. I repeat, we'll be comin' ashore tomorrow unless we hear back from you.

Hayley dropped the sandwich she had been holding. "No," she whispered hoarsely. Tomorrow morning? That was too soon—much too soon. She hadn't even begun to make plans for a shelter and hiding spot. She hated to think about what would happen if she was caught. I should've just drowned with Jack. Then I wouldn't be in this mess.

With a heavy heart, she resumed her meager lunch. She was almost done licking the peanut butter off her fingers when a sudden crackling made her freeze. Something told her it wasn't the radio again. This time it sounded like a stick had been broken.

Like someone was walking through the jungle.

Panic seized Hayley's limbs. She willed herself to move, to sprint away from the clearing, to do something, but her legs wouldn't cooperate. Her brain automatically made the connection between the unmanned boat and the sound she now heard. Who could it be?

She watched wide-eyed in the direction of the noise. Yes, someone was definitely coming. Was it really her rescuer? Or were Clyde's men lying when they said they would wait until tomorrow morning? Hayley cursed her gullibility. She knew she was smarter than that.

Suddenly, in the middle of her panicked thoughts, a lone silhouette appeared on the edge of the clearing. All of Hayley's hairs stood on end. Run! Run, you idiot!

But when the figure stepped into view, her adrenaline dissolved into confusion. She didn't know whether to cry out of relief or run a spear through her heart. Were Jack's death, Billings' corpse, and the mysterious island driving her insane?

No, they weren't. She knew, as her fingers relaxed their grip into the dirt and her body ceased to shake, that she was perfectly fine. She was sane. She was even rescued.

But of all the people, it had to be Oliver?

Chapter 36

The two classmates stared at each other for what seemed like hours, when in reality it was a mere half-minute. Oliver broke the silence. "Hayley?"

"Oliver?" she cried.

The spell was broken. They rushed forward and collapsed in each other's arms, Hayley sobbing with relief and Oliver smiling like a fool.

"My God," Hayley murmured into his shoulder, "you have no idea how glad I am to see you."

Oliver just patted her on the back. "I could say the same."

She pulled away and wiped her tears. "So how did you know I was here? How did you find me? Is Gran worried?"

"Listen." Oliver sat with one leg outstretched, his hands folded in his lap. His gaze dropped to the ground. "Um, I'm sorry, Hayley, but I kind of followed you on The Queen Francis."

Hayley almost laughed out loud. "Do you think that matters now? I'm finally rescued! I don't care if you've been following me my whole life—I'm finally getting out of this Godforsaken place!"

"No." Oliver wanted to reach out and grab one of her hands, but he restrained himself. "Hayley, listen. I followed you, and I'm sorry. I stayed out of your way the entire boat trip, but when I heard that you had gone missing, I felt like it was partly my fault."

"Your fault?" she echoed dumbly.

"If I had shown my face instead of hiding like a coward, I might have saved you." He blushed.

"Oh, Oliver...do you really think that? These men—treasure hunters—kidnapped me. There was nothing you could do. And it was really all my fault, since I wandered into the jungle in the first place. Then one thing led to another, and Jack and I were linked, and we started wandering all over this island for clues—"

Oliver's puzzled look stopped her.

"Sorry. I guess I should start from the beginning."

"Please," he said.

She let out a deep sigh. "Look, there are a lot of things we both need to say. We have a lot of catching up to do, but I think it's only fair that I start."

"Hayley—" he began, but she shushed him.

"I'm sorry for treating you the way I have." Now it was Hayley's turn to stare at the ground, ashamed. Oliver was stunned speechless. "I was easily annoyed and I wanted to cut my time with you short. That isn't fair, and I'm so sorry. You mean well, Oliver, and in return all I've done is play the hypocrite."

He opened and closed his mouth, unsure of what to say. With Hayley's red cheeks streaked with tears, her dirty skin and clothes, and her ragged appearance, she looked miserable. Oliver pitied her.

"I forgive you," he said awkwardly.

A ghost of a smile slipped onto her face. "Good," she breathed.

"I'm sorry if I annoy you. I—I guess—I just want to spend time with you." He stumbled over the words, not sure how they would be received.

"Anything," Hayley said. "I'll do anything in return for you rescuing me." She clasped one of his hands and smiled gratefully.

Oliver shifted uncomfortably on the hard ground. Wasn't his stomach supposed to flutter and his hand become sweaty? He was finally holding hands with Hayley Slade, and yet nothing was happening! "Um," he replied, "well, I guess you're wondering how I found you...?"

"Yes!"

And so, for the next hour, the pair shared sandwiches and water bottles while they traded stories. Hayley's misfortunes were bared once again, and no matter how hard she tried not to cry, describing them to Oliver was like peeling off a new scab. His gentle touch and warm smile were comforting, but it was his own tale that appalled her.

When news of Hayley's disappearance had reached the media, Oliver explained, the police were onto it right away. The investigation was kept under wraps, but multiple theories continued to float around. Ultimately, the search was fruitless, mainly due to the sheer size of the Caribbean. It wasn't like the coast guard could simply travel across every square foot of the sea.

That's when Oliver knew he had to do something. "It came to me," he'd said, "after class one day when I saw your number in my contacts. I tracked your phone through the GPS, which led me to that big boat anchored offshore this island." He went on to say how he wasted no time in renting a boat from a sympathetic Jamaican dealer and heading straight for the GPS coordinates. When he realized they led straight to the Antonia, he wisely stayed out of sight and watched the men on the boat through binoculars. He had recognized them as the group aboard The Queen Francis and quickly put two and two together. As soon as it was nightfall, he cruised into the bay, anchored his own boat, and swam ashore. He had wandered through the jungle until daylight, when he spotted a thin trail of smoke. The smoke, which was from the bonfire, led him to the clearing where Hayley was.

Oliver's tale made Hayley view him in a different light, but more importantly, she picked out the single flaw he had made. "So it's your boat that's anchored in the bay?" she asked.

"Yes."

She groaned. "Oliver! It's broad daylight, and now the men on the Antonia know you're here! They were radioing Clyde all day, warning him about an 'unmanned boat' and promising to come ashore in the morning if they didn't hear back from him."

Oliver winced. "I know anchoring my boat in the bay was a bad move, but I had no other options. This entire island is surrounded by rocks!"

Hayley pursed her lips. "You're right. But now we have to move—and fast. The last thing we should do is stay right here where the smoke is. This is exactly where the men will look first, just like you did." Adrenaline flowed through her veins. Whether it was due to Oliver's arrival or the imminent danger of Clyde's men, she suddenly felt empowered. Her period of grieving was over, and it was time to take charge. "Come on," she said, grabbing Oliver's hand. "Grab a few backpacks and let's get outta here."

Hayley was on autopilot. Her thoughts were consumed with survival and how to elude the bad guys. Oliver's labored breathing, coupled with his loud steps as he stumbled through the jungle, only fueled the need to escape. Hayley was so close to getting off the island that she would do anything she could to stay alive.

After nearly a week of traversing the island, she now felt fairly confident in getting around. She led Oliver to the Silver River, where they drank and rested for a few minutes. Few words were spoken, and soon it was time to head towards the bay. Hayley had grabbed Clyde's backpack before leaving the clearing, but wisely turned the volume of his radio down. The men on the Antonia hadn't radioed yet, however. Hayley hated not knowing their plans. Were they preparing to go ashore at the very minute, or would they wait until morning like they'd said?

The temperature was finally cooling down by the time Hayley and Oliver reached the bay. She could tell he was eager to jump into the cool water. "Wait," she said softly. They crouched in the thick foliage of the jungle and peered through two palm fronds at the Antonia. Its hull glittered in the bright sunlight. Even closer was Oliver's smaller boat, which appeared to have been ransacked and searched by Clyde's men.

Hayley rummaged through Clyde's backpack and pulled out his binoculars. "I don't see anyone," she said after looking for a few minutes.

"Maybe they're already on the island," Oliver suggested.

"They would have radioed Clyde." She fingered the radio, unsure of what to do. "Or maybe they figured the people on the other boat—your boat—ran into Clyde, and he was in trouble."

"But after ransacking my boat, Clyde's men would be able to tell that my provisions are enough for only one person."

"Okay, so they're expecting just one guy, then. They know he's somewhere on the island—"

Oliver grinned cheekily.

"—and they figured this guy ran into Clyde. Maybe that's why they haven't radioed Clyde: they were afraid the sailor was in possession of Clyde's radio."

"It's a thought," Oliver said.

"Well, whatever's going on, we can't take off until we know where they are."

And so the waiting began. Oliver and Hayley remained still for half an hour, sometimes expecting Clyde's lackeys to burst out of the foliage behind them at any moment. Hayley was tempted to circle back to the clearing and see if they had left any tracks. She still didn't know if they were already on the island or still waiting for Clyde in the Antonia.

Sweat trickled down her back. All she wanted to do was go home. Escape was so close...

"There!" Oliver nearly shouted, scaring Hayley out of her skin.

"What? Where?"

Oliver, who had been looking through the binocs, passed them to Hayley. "They were on the Antonia this whole time. They're just getting into a rowboat now."

Hayley looked and realized Oliver was right. "Let's hope they see the smoke and go to the opposite side of the bay. If they come towards us, we run."

They watched breathlessly as Clyde's remaining three men slowly rowed into shore. Once they set foot on the sand, their beady eyes scanned the jungle, passing directly over Hayley and Oliver's hiding spot. Suddenly, one of the men gave a sharp cry, and their attention was directed to the thin plume of smoke rising in the air. Hayley breathed a sigh of relief as they headed to the opposite side of the bay.

"They're leaving!" Oliver cried in relief. Hayley shushed him.

"Give them some time. We need to be sure they're long gone before making our great escape." Those two words tasted magnificent on Hayley's tongue. She couldn't help but smile. We're almost there...

Five minutes later, Hayley crept towards the fringe of the jungle and took a tentative step onto the sand. She held her breath and scanned the bay for any sign of a scout Clyde's men had left behind. It appeared all three had gone to the clearing.

"Let's go," she said, giving Oliver a thumbs-up.

He grabbed his backpacks and darted out of the hiding spot. Together, they rushed towards the water and made a beeline for Oliver's boat. Hayley suddenly paused waist-deep in the surf. "I'll meet you by the Antonia," she said.

"What?"

She pointed at the rowboat left behind by the three men. "Shouldn't we strand them on the island?"

Oliver cocked his head to one side. "It's up to you."

Hayley needed no further advice. She waded back onto shore, pushed the rowboat into the water, and headed out to sea. Marooning Clyde's men wasn't an ethical problem to her, despite the fact that the island had no source of food. If they died, so be it. Hayley figured when she was back in Florida, she could always tell the coast guard where the men were.

Her arms burned and ached by the time she made it to Clyde's boat. Oliver reminded her that they needed to hoist the rowboat on deck before anything else. "We'll take the Antonia back to the mainland," he said. "It's bigger and faster. Then we can pull mine behind it. Is that alright with you?"

"As long as we get out of here in one piece," she said.

As Oliver helped her aboard the Antonia, his attention was suddenly diverted back to the island. "What the—?"

Hayley stumbled onto the deck. "Huh?"

Oliver just gawked at the bay. "Um...I could be wrong, but I don't think that's one of the bad guys. Do you know who it is?"

Hayley peered at the lone figure jumping up and down on shore, waving his arms frantically. Her heart jumped into her throat and her knees buckled. "Oh my God..." Her walls suddenly came crashing down. Her survival instincts, which had fed off her adrenaline, plummeted from her thoughts. She was so overwhelmed she didn't know whether to cry, laugh, or simply stare in disbelief.

"Hayley, who is that?" Oliver asked again.

She finally snapped out of her trance and grabbed both of Oliver's arms. "It's him—he's alive!" Without waiting for an answer, she dove into the water, climbed onto Oliver's boat, and headed to shore. Once she was in shallow water, she stopped and jumped out. She was a smiling, splashing mess when she stumbled into Jack's arms. His grip was frail and weak, his body reeking of salt and sweat, but to Hayley he was just as perfect as ever. He was alive, and that was all that mattered.

Epilogue

T WO MONTHS LATER

Hayley sat on the wooden dock, swinging her legs lazily over the blue-green water as she stared into the sunset. Her camera dangled from its strap around her neck, exactly where it should be. On her left was Gran, who had a half-smile on her wrinkled face; and on Hayley's right was tall, skinny Oliver.

Things had finally quieted down after Hayley, Oliver, and Jack returned to Palmetto Bay. After numerous interviews, both in newspapers and on television (all of which Jack had avoided), the case of the missing persons Hayley Slade, Clyde Pickett, and the rest of the men came to a close. The coast guard had planned to use Oliver's coordinates to return to the shell-shaped island, but those coordinates had been inconveniently erased and Hayley's cell phone unfortunately destroyed. Thus the treasure was kept secret.

The story Hayley told to the press was this: she had wandered into the jungle during one of The Queen Francis' island stops, where she accidentally ran into Clyde's men. They were planning a treasure hunt, and since Hayley had heard valuable information, they kidnapped her. Jack had been stuck in the same scenario months earlier and stranded on another island. From there, minus all the magical clues and actual discovery of the treasure, the rest was the same: Oliver rescued Hayley, they found Jack, and they returned home.

Though this story fascinated the public, Jack's tale of how he'd escaped from the blowhole—which he told to Hayley in private—was even more appalling. The current flowing from the tidepool to the blowhole had sucked him inside the cave, as Hayley had thought. Jack described it as being pulled in all directions and tumbled like a ragdoll in a washing machine. He had been thrown against the walls of the cave multiple times until he was bloodied and disoriented. Just as he had been sucked up towards the sharp spikes leading to the blowhole, the current ceased to flow, and the waters receded. As Jack's limp body sank to the bottom, the cave slowly became a pool again, and there he had lain amid the blood and gore of Clyde and his men.

Once Jack came to, he had gathered all his strength and swam back through the tunnel and up to the tidepool. He had lain in the sand weak, bloodied, and bruised, but eventually made his way to the clearing, where he had eaten leftover food and drank some water from the men's backpacks.

"We must have just missed each other," Jack told Hayley afterwards. "I probably arrived at the clearing after you and Oliver had already left. The sandwiches and water built up my strength a bit, so when I suddenly heard three of Clyde's men marching through the jungle, I ran. I headed straight for the bay, and that's when I saw you in the boat."

Once again, Hayley was astounded at Jack's strength and will to survive. After they returned to Palmetto Bay, Hayley's life resumed as normal. She went to college, worked on her photography portfolio, and (reluctantly) continued her job at Coco's as a waitress. She especially enjoyed her time with Gran. If anything, their separation had brought them even closer together.

"I knew that boat trip was good for you!" Gran had exulted one evening when they were sitting in front of her new HD TV (a hard-fought victory for Hayley).

"Good for me?" Hayley had echoed, her jaw dropping in surprise. "I was kidnapped, for heavens' sake!"

"Besides that, honey. All bad things aside, you had the experience of a lifetime as well as the opportunity to meet two very handsome young men." Gran winked.

Now, as Hayley sat on the dock, her cheeks flushed with remembrance. Oliver she couldn't imagine as "handsome." He was too awkward; too lanky. He meant well, but he wasn't her type.

And Jack...? Hayley almost groaned. If truth be told, "handsome" was an understatement for the boy who used to have a crush on her in high school.

Gran suddenly reached over and wrapped her leathery fingers around Hayley's hand. The two smiled. Yes, life was almost back to the way it was. After she had returned to Palmetto Bay, Hayley felt terrible for Jack, who had no home to return to. So Hayley had moved in with Gran and let Jack stay in her apartment until he found a job. Two months had gone by, though, and without a college education and certain legal documents, work was hard to come by.

"Hayley," Oliver said suddenly, shattering her out of her thoughts. More often than not, her mind was stuck in the past. "Can I tell you something?" he asked.

She nodded and withdrew her hand from Gran's. Oliver led her down the dock and into the parking lot, where they stood and watched the boats bobbing in the marina. He cleared his throat. "School will be over in less than a month, you know."

"Yeah," Hayley said lamely.

"I don't think I'm coming back."

She turned to face him, startled. "What?"

"I feel like I'm wasting my time." Oliver fidgeted and stuck his hands in his pockets. "With college, I mean. I like photography, and I used to want to major in math—"

"I thought you had trouble with math."

"Oh...er, well..." He scratched his head uncomfortably. "I guess that's changed now. I realize what I'm doing studying at FIU isn't what I want to be doing for the rest of my life."

"And what's that?"

Oliver blushed. "A counselor."

"Like a school counselor?" Hayley couldn't help but smile. "You've certainly got the patience and kindness."

"Florida's become too rushed for me. I don't like the fast pace of life," he continued. "What I really want to live is somewhere up north—Oregon, perhaps, or maybe Washington."

"Oh." Somehow Hayley felt like a part of herself was leaving along with Oliver. "If that's what you want to do..."

"Yeah." He fidgeted again. "Um, listen, Hayley...I like you. You're really kind and sweet and"—here he blushed—"pretty. I hate to leave you and FIU, but this is what feels right to me. Otherwise I'm just going through the motions."

"I understand." Hayley squeezed his hand. "Don't let me hold you back. But do stay in touch, okay?"

"Okay." He smiled goofily. "Well, uh, I guess I'll see in class tomorrow."

She nodded and watched as he headed towards his car, his long strides widening the distance between them. She fingered her camera strap absentmindedly. Just then, a thought came to her. "Oliver—wait!"

He turned around.

"Hey, I forgot to ask you: ever since you found me on the island, you haven't stuttered once."

Oliver was silent for a half-minute, pondering her words. Then a wide grin spread across his face. "I don't know," he finally admitted. "I guess this whole experience has changed me. I think I'm more confident."

"That's great, Oliver!"

"Yeah, well, sometimes my stuttering accidentally s-slips out." He chuckled, waved, and headed back to his car.

Hayley laughed softly as well. Good old Oliver.

Her footfalls were light as she walked down the dock towards Gran. She stared between the cracks of the wooden planks at the dark seawater below. Goosebumps sprouted on her arms. When she glanced up, she was surprised to see someone sitting next to Gran. The elderly lady smiled as she talked animatedly to her visitor.

Hayley quickened her pace and grinned when she realized who it was. "Hey!"

"Long time no see," Jack said, giving her a wide smile. He scooted over to give her some room to sit down, which she did.

"So how did the interview go?" she asked, referring to how Jack had sought a job as a construction worker that afternoon.

He shook his head. "It's hopeless. No one is going to hire me."

Gran let out a sigh and carefully got to her feet. Hayley helped her up, confusion written across her features. "Where are you going?"

"Jack has some big news he needs to tell you. I think I'll leave you two for a bit and meet you back at the car." She smiled and winked.

Hayley's confusion peaked. She turned to Jack. "What big news? I thought you didn't get the job."

"See, that's the problem." Once Gran was a good distance down the dock, he scooted closer and grabbed Hayley's hand. "Listen, I appreciate how much you and your grandmother have done for me. It's more than I could ever ask—a home, opportunities for work, and a temporary family."

Hayley smiled softly. "But...?"

"But I think it's time I move on."

"Jack, you can't—"

"It's my decision," he said firmly. "I have nothing against you or your grandmother, believe me. It's just that I've been on the run for so many years, it doesn't feel right to stay in one place for so long."

"It's only been two months." Hayley felt him already slipping away as they spoke. "You haven't found a job...how will you get food and water? Where will you live? How—"

"I've done it before, and I can do it again." Jack stood up and helped Hayley to her feet. She was shocked when he pulled her into an embrace. "Listen," he murmured into her hair, "I'm not leaving forever. I'll be back in the summer, I promise. Most likely I won't even leave Florida."

Hayley nodded, though tears were now brimming in her eyes. "You should have given me notice, Jack. I...I don't know what to say."

"I'm leaving tonight." He pulled away and placed both of his hands on her shoulders.

"Are you sure?"

"Positive."

Hayley bit her lip. Why was he leaving now all of a sudden? Why had been Gran been smiling when she talked with him? "Is that all you wanted to tell me?"

He grinned. "Not at all."

"Is it about your ancestor?"

Now it was Jack's turn to be confused. "Uh...no."

"Remember the morning when we found the golden water, and we traded stories?"

He nodded.

"You never did tell me who your pirate ancestor was."

"Hayley, honest to God, you don't want to know."

"It's been bugging me for two months. I do want to know."

He groaned. After a few moments of mental debate, he caved. "Fine. His name was Jean-David Nau, more famously known as François l'Olonnais."

It suddenly clicked. "He was French," Hayley said. "Is that why the map in our heads contained French clues?"

"Most likely. Even though Nau first came to the Caribbean as an indentured servant, he broke free and became one of the most ruthless pirates of the seventeenth century. In a nutshell, he sacked the Spanish town of Maracaibo, tortured and killed its residents, and even cut open the chest of one of the Spanish soldiers and gnawed on his heart."

Hayley shuddered.

"Nau was an expert torturer, but he came to a fitting end. After leaving Maracaibo, his crew ran aground on a shoal near Panama, ran into some natives, and were eaten."

"Yikes."

"You can see why I don't like talking about it."

Hayley stared down at the wooden planks of the dock, thoughtful. "Thanks for telling me, Jack. Did the pirate bury his treasure from Maracaibo on the shell-shaped island, then?"

"Yes. I don't know why he would bury his treasure except maybe because his ship was bogged down and overflowing. Aside from Maracaibo, he sacked a good number of other towns as well."

"Do you know how the map appeared in his descendants' minds? And how did it come to be in my mind, too?"

"Honestly, I don't know," Jack admitted. "All I remember from the genealogy written underneath my mother's drawer"—here Hayley smiled—"was that every descendant of Jean-David Nau had the map in their head. It took me years to discover it, though, and when I did, I only saw half of it."

"But when you linked with me, I could see the other half, thus completing the clue."

"Exactly."

"Amazing," Hayley breathed. She wanted to reach out, hold Jack's hand, and close her eyes, but they had already tried that several times since returning home. Once they had found the treasure, the map in their heads was gone. Vanished.

Jack fidgeted for a moment, uncertainty shadowing his features. "I think there's another reason why you were able to complete the map for me."

"I'm listening."

"Look, don't take this the wrong way, but..." He touched her shoulder. "I don't believe it was possible for me to link with anyone else. It took a certain person to make that connection, and you were perfect."

Hayley didn't know what to say. "You mean...?"

"Yeah." He removed his hand from her shoulder and cleared his throat. The contact they had, brief though it was, made both hearts beat a little faster. "I could be wrong," Jack concluded, "but that's my theory. Anyway, I'm very sorry about leaving, but I have to prove myself. I have to break away from the horrors my ancestor committed. This is just something I feel like I have to do. I promise I'll be back in the summer."

"But why leave and come back when you can stay?"

"I might try to track down my mom. Maybe even my dad, if both of them are still alive." His eyes swam with sadness, so he quickly changed topics. "But on a happier note, I'm leaving because I need some time and supplies."

"For...?"

"How does a visit to our favorite shell-shaped island sound?"

Hayley's jaw dropped open. "Are you saying what I think you're saying?"

Jack's eyes twinkled. "We know where the treasure is. We just need to go back and see where it washed out through that hole in the cave."

"Oh, Jack, I'd love to! But Oliver got rid of the coordinates. We won't be able to find the island again."

"Did he?" Jack winked. "Or did he just say that to get the media off our backs?"

Hayley laughed. "And here I was, hoping to never see another deserted island again in my life!"

Jack suddenly leaned forward and brushed his lips across her forehead. "To the island it is, then."

Hayley felt sparks shooting from the top of her head to the soles of her feet. "Wait, Jack—before you go." She walked around to the other side of him, so that he was in between her and the blazing sunset. "Stay still."

"What—?"

She lifted her camera, adjusted the aperture and shutter speed, and snapped a photo. "There," she said, satisfied.

Jack smiled. "I'll be back soon, Hayley Slade."

It was bittersweet, watching Jack's muscled form stroll down the dock and disappear into the darkness. Thankfully, Hayley didn't cry, nor did she give in to the temptation to chase after him. She heaved a sigh and looked at the picture she had just taken. Jack's silhouette, fringed by the beautiful orange and pink sky, would have to suffice for the next few months.

She turned off her camera and looked at the sunset one last time. "See you soon, Jack."

www.ingramcontent.com/pod-product-compliance
Lightning Source LLC
Chambersburg PA
CBHW070946190726
48292CB00004B/1346